THE BELIEVE GENE:
Obsession and Cherry Pie

Sally Ramsey

ISBN – 978-1-949802-30-6
LCCN - 2023939153
Published by Black Pawn Press

FIRST EDITION

TO ALL THE PARENTS WHO FIGHT FOR
THEIR CHILDREN'S FUTURES.

CHAPTER ONE

THE EIGHTIES

To women in early pregnancy, Emend-No seemed like a godsend. It banished morning sickness and filled them with energy. There was no reason to believe the drug could cause any harm to a child in the womb. The animal tests showed indication of trouble, and the level of birth defects observed was no higher than statistical norms. If the I.Q.s of the babies born of mothers who took it skewed a bit low, the change was still within the range of error. With their medication a considerable success and major seller, Ober-Bio Pharmaceuticals enjoyed a steady stream of profits.

Low-Dunn Chemical became the star of the New York Stock Exchange and the darling of agribusiness. Its herbicide cut costs and waste for farmers across the country. Homeowners are breathed a sigh of relief as weekends, once lost to battling weeds, were freed up for family time and enjoying sports on new color TVs. Their kids had a few more colds and allergies, but not enough to worry their pediatricians. Memories of the war receded, the economy was recovering, and optimism ruled the airwaves.

1992

Ten-year-old Chester Taxtrum beats his little fists against the kitchen table. "Denny and Charlie are liars. I hate them!"

Fingers curled around her wooden spoon, Mary Taxtrum tries to keep her white sauce from burning while calming her son. "They're your best friends. I'm sure they didn't mean to lie to you. What did they say?"

"That Santa Claus doesn't bring Christmas presents, that he isn't real."

Mary stares at her son in confusion. "But you know that Daddy and I bought you your bike. You helped pick it out. And Grandma took you to buy your new jacket."

Chester's flushed skin takes on a purplish cast. "You are just helpers! Santa drives his sleigh to the house of every good child in the world. He comes down the chimney and puts the gifts under the tree."

"Chester," Mary gently reminds her son, "we don't have a chimney."

A table leg splinters under assault from Chester's sneaker-covered feet. "Santa's magic. He makes chimneys. He can do anything. You and Daddy are fake helpers!"

Mary hurriedly turns off the heat under her failing sauce to chase after her frantic son.

1993

"What is your concern about your son, Mrs. Taxtrum?" Doctor Bellamy inquires.

Grasping the handle of her purse as the only thing she can cling to, Mary gazes at the bland expression of the psychologist Chester's school recommended. "I guess you'd say he's stubborn. He gets these crazy ideas in his head, and no matter what anyone says or does, he won't change his mind."

"What kind of ideas?" Bellamy asks.

"He decided that the moon landing was faked. When his teacher tried to tell him it was real and that her brother worked on it at NASA, he trashed everything on her desk. The principal suspended him to two weeks and sent him home with a book on the space program. Chester claimed it was all lies and tore it up."

"How was your pregnancy with Chester, Mrs. Taxtrum?"

Mary's eyes flash. "Why would you need to know that?"

"We've found that sometimes when women remember having a difficult time carrying them, the children sense it and act out."

"He'd have no reason to do that," Mary protests. "The minute I started feeling sick, my doctor gave me Emend-No, and I sailed right through."

"How about exercise?" Bellamy inquires. "Often, boys need to blow off some steam. Does Chester get to run around outside?"

"He runs around our yard for hours," Mary claims. "A couple of years ago, we lived in an apartment, and he was such a sweet child. But my husband and I thought we should have a house with a backyard. Chester has a swing set and monkey bars. And Henry keeps the grass perfect for playing on. He makes sure there isn't a weed anywhere. But it seems the more time Chester spends out there, the worse he gets."

"In that case, I'll need you to bring him in for some tests, so I can determine what kind of therapy he needs," Bellamy explains.

Mary sighs. "And how long will therapy take?"

Bellamy leans earnestly across his desk. "I'm afraid there's no way we can know that. You can make an appointment outside."

2016

Cautiously pleased to see Chester Taxtrum come through the door of Guns a Plenty, Wade Meacham flashes an ingratiating smile. "Welcome back. What can I get for you today?"

Chester surveys the weapons displayed on the wall and in glass cases. "I wish I could buy out the whole damn store, but my asshole boss just cut my hours. All I could scrape together is $500. But if this country is stupid enough to elect that bitch, she'll be coming to our doors to take away our God-given right to bear arms. We have to defend ourselves. I need a pistol I can keep on my hip. What's the best you've got for me?"

"You got here just in time," Meacham declares. "Lots of folks are thinking the way you are. A Springfield Armory Hellcat is the best you can buy for that price, but I only have one left. If you don't grab it, it'll be gone in 10 minutes."

Chester pulls a roll of bills out of his back pocket. "That weapon is mine."

As he studies the postings in his Facebook group, Chester strokes the grip of his new defense against the evil threatening to overtake his homeland. The bitch is even worse than he thought. He always knew she was a whore, but now she's turning kids into sex slaves. He can't let it happen. To take out her operation, he'll need more than his Hellcat. Who knows how many minions she's lured into her evil flock? He needs his Bushmaster to bring them down like the animals they are. The center of the bitch's operations is 600 miles away, but he can drive that in a day, easy. He can raid his emergency stocks for everything he'll need to get there without stopping. For the good of the country, Chester will make the assault that will bring her down.

From her place in a circle of mothers in her church basement, Mary Taxtrum rises shakily to her feet. "If you saw the news, you know what my son did. He walked into a family restaurant with an assault weapon, thinking he was taking down a child trafficking ring he heard about on the internet. I hate to believe it, but I do.

"I'm like all of you. I have a child who insists on the most ridiculous things and doesn't seem capable of listening to reason. We've all been supporting each other. But I think we need to do more than that. At least I do. I need to know why Chester did what he did and if there's anything I can do to prevent things like that from happening again. So I'm asking if any of you are willing to help me find out."

Lily Rostoff pushes out of her chair. "Every time I see my son, he has a gun and says something crazy. It could have been Evan instead of Chester. I want in. But what can I do to help? What do you want me or any of us to do?"

"Look, we come from different backgrounds, races, jobs. It seems like we have nothing in common but our kids. But they must have something connecting them to each other. We need to find out what it is," Mary asserts. "These days, everything is about D.N.A. Our children could have some weird gene. So maybe we can have their genomes sequenced and compared."

Lily shakes her head. "Evan thinks we're the ones who don't know what's going on, and there's nothing wrong with him. He'll never let me get his D.N.A."

"Chester is out on bail, but he won't either," Mary agrees. "We'll have to be creative. Would you all be okay with inviting an expert to our next meeting?" Heads bob around the circle, and Mary knows that she's going to war.

CHAPTER TWO

The terms of Chester's bail don't allow him to leave the state where he was arrested, so Mary spends the better part of two days driving to see him. He's willing to see her, if for no other reason than she promised to bring him much-needed cash and some stuff from his apartment. Packing up his things allowed her to figure out the best way to get a D.N.A. sample. She feels like a sneak but buys one of each color of the kind of toothbrushes he's using. He chose the brand hawked by his favorite radio personality when he was in high school and never changed. The friend who works in the crime lab she invited to her support group said that a fresh sample of cells from the mouth can produce a good D.N.A. profile. A toothbrush is the best way Mary can think of to get them.

When Mary arrives at the tiny apartment Chester rented temporarily, she's surprised to find him in a good mood. He explains that he's proud to be standing up for what he believes. And an organization he hooked up with online will be picking up his legal fees. Mary isn't sure whether to celebrate or cry, so she settles for giving her son the things she brought, a hug, and figuring out how she'll manage to get any rest on his couch that night.

Mary has no trouble knowing that Chester is asleep. She suspects his neighbors have no problem either. He'd occasionally been a noisy sleeper as a child. But the volume of his snoring increased through his teen years. She was ashamed at her relief when he was out of the house. Mary finds his toothbrush easily enough and switches it out for the red one she brought, carefully preserving her sample the way her friend instructed.

The analysis won't be cheap. If she were tracing her ancestors, a lab would be looking only for specific markers and charge a lot less. But since Mary has no idea what genes might be involved, her lab will have to sequence everything. That means she'll have to dig into some of the insurance money she got when Henry died. But if she can find out what's going on with Chester, it will be worth it.

Chester is enthusiastic about eating the French toast Mary manages to pull together from the sparse contents of his refrigerator, but not about having her stay. She does her best to avoid mentioning politics. But they both know that they might as well live on different planets for the way they view events in the country. The more time they spend together, the more pronounced the differences in their outlooks become. Chester sees his mother as naïve, at best, and she sees him as falling for scam artists.

Mary decides to take off after breakfast but seeks out the privacy of the bathroom to call Lily Rostoff before she leaves. "Did you get Chester's D.N.A.?" Lily demands.

Mary finds herself nodding, even on the phone. "I did. Did you get Evan's?"

"Not yet, but we're meeting for coffee this afternoon. I'm going to try to get a cup or a napkin or something."

"Good luck. Listen," Mary adds. "I'm going to overnight Chester's sample to the lab from here while it's still fresh. I figure if they find something unusual in his genome, they can just look for a match to it from Evan. That would be cheaper and faster."

"I don't care if it's cheaper," Lily claims. "I just want some answers."

"So do I," Mary agrees. "Send your sample off as soon as you can, but we'll have to wait some time for results. I'll let you know they minute I hear anything."

"Same here," Lily responds. "Mary, we're doing the right thing, aren't we?"

A sigh forces itself from Mary's mouth. "I don't see how we can do anything else. Talk to you soon."

As she slogs through the week, Mary finds it harder to concentrate on her job. Usually, she finds working in one of the few toy stores left satisfying. She winces at the occasional piercing screams when a desperately wanted toy is out of stock or a harried parent says no, but on most days, skipping feet come to her, conveying blissful smiles. Gazing at the excitement of the joyful children, she remembers Chester the way he was before the change. As she waits for the results of Chester's D.N.A. analysis, the troubled years weigh on her life a barbell across her shoulders.

After checking her mail daily for a written report, Mary's surprised to get a call from a Doctor Lawrence. He teaches at a University over 2,000 miles away in California. "Mrs. Taxtrum, the sample you sent to your local facility was passed on to me because it may fit into a genetics investigation my team is carrying out. The D.N.A. can't be yours because it is obviously male, and privacy demands that I only have an identification number for it, but we've found some unusual characteristics that we find relevant. Can you tell me if the D.N.A. is from an individual diagnosed with cognitive impairment or developmental disability of some kind?"

Mary feels her chest tighten. "I can tell you that he had a battery of tests as a child but never received a diagnosis of either. He has other problems, though."

For a moment, Lawrence says nothing. "Ms. Taxtrum, the reason I'm asking is that we found what are referred to as deletions in a gene often associated with the emotional responses to new information. I can also tell you that this type of deletion is sometimes seen in the children of mothers who took a drug sold as Emend-No during pregnancy."

"His mother took Emend-No, but it was supposed to be perfectly safe," Mary protests.

"By itself, that has seemed true. However, until recently, the interaction of genes with environmental factors wasn't understood," Lawrence explains. "Some genes are active until silenced by a process called methylation. Our team is investigating what could cause the deactivation of that gene and the resulting effects. Would you mind if I send you are questionnaire regarding possible exposures of the person to whom this sample belongs?"

"Please send it, Doctor Lawrence. Um," Mary continues, "I'm involved with a support group for parents of children with behaviors similar to the person whose D.N.A. profile you received. Would it make sense if they filled out questionnaires as well?"

Mary can hear a sharp intake of breath, "Ms. Taxtrum, that would make a great deal of sense. The questionnaires will be coded to ensure identification with continued privacy. Give me your address. You'll have them tomorrow."

As soon as Lawrence hangs up, Mary calls Lily Rostoff. "I think we may be getting somewhere. Listen to this…"

CHAPTER THREE

"What's the emergency?" Millie Robb asks as Mary goes to the center of the chair circle with a stack of Dr. Lawrence's questionnaires.

"Not an emergency, but finally something we can do besides talk," Mary explains. "Do you remember the consultant at our meeting last month? I did what she said and got a sample of Chester's D.N.A."

"I got Evan's, too," Lily adds.

"I guess labs talk to each other or something, but a Doctor Lawrence in California saw something about Chester's genome that could help explain why our kids are the way they are. He's just starting to figure it out, and these questionnaires will help him. You don't have to put your names on them or anything. Just fill them out about your kids," Mary requests. "And I'll send them back."

"What's this about Emend-No?" Frieda Beckenstein asks. "I took that when I was pregnant with Michael, but the doctor said it was safe."

"A lot of women still take it," Marg Newberg interjects. "Some of my friends took it when they were pregnant, and their kids are fine. This checklist is just more useless crap."

"It isn't!" Mary insists. "Doctor Lawrence said that the problem involves something besides Emend-No. He's trying to figure out what. That's what these surveys are for."

"Those damn doctors don't know shit!" Marg proclaims. "Nothing a doctor's said has ever helped me with Alan. You can all fill those papers out if you want, but I'm not wasting my time. If you ladies start making sense, maybe I'll see you next month."

Several other women follow Marg through a heavy wooden door that slams behind them. Mary sinks into a folding chair, the metal chilling her back. "Then I guess it's just us. I have extra pens if anyone needs one. We'll have a lot to write. Lily, did you bring any of the good white cookies? We can use the energy."

Lily pulls a round metal can with a poinsettia on it from a canvas tote. "Got them right here."

"How many people turned in their questionnaire?" Lily asks after the meeting breaks up.

Mary does a quick count. "Ten. I hope that's enough." She picks up a pre-addressed express mail envelope and begins to insert the forms.

"What if they get lost or something?" Lily wonders. "We had enough trouble getting people to do them once. They're not going to do them again. We should make copies, just in case."

"Right," Mary agrees. "If we hurry, I can still get these in a drop box before the pick-up time today." She strides towards the meeting room door. "Let's do it."

After sending off the questionnaires to Doctor Lawrence, Mary flips through the copies. Lawrence regarded the information as private, so she really shouldn't be reading it, but Mary knows the people in her group. She understands their anguish better than Lawrence or anyone who doesn't have child like theirs could, so she needs to know if what she just did will mean anything.

She skims through the responses. Damn! Lawrence was right about Emend-No. All the moms took it, but there has to be something else they have in common. The second section is about any changes in family life before the onset of symptoms. A few moved to the suburbs like she did. For the rest, their children already had a place to play outside. When they got out of hand, all the kids were getting the fresh air and sunshine that was supposed to be good for them. The problem couldn't just be playing outside. Some of the kids had been doing it for years. There has to be something else.

Mary wishes she could ask Henry. He knew everything he used to keep the yard beautiful, but she had a gardener take over after losing him. She hadn't touched Henry's shed since then. It could be past time. Maybe Lawrence suspects some chemical of causing Chester's crazy behavior. She hopes so.

When Mary gets home, she enters the small structure that had been her husband's private domain. It's full of boxes and bags, some of which she can hardly lift. She can't help but notice the paragraphs of small print on most of the products. It makes sense in a way. They were formulated to kill various threats to Henry's dream of a perfect yard. Almost anything designed to kill pests in the house displays a prominent warning to keep it out of the reach of children. Yet Chester and she'd guess so many other youngsters, happily played on stretches of green loaded with all kinds of garden chemicals. Henry never would have used anything he thought could harm Chester, but maybe the manufacturers were less than forthcoming. Or maybe, like the pharmaceutical company making Emend-No, their tests said they had nothing to worry about.

Mary decides to try a web search for anyone asking the same questions she is. Returning to the house, she gets a notebook and a pen to take down the name of every product that Henry left behind. She checks her watch. She has an evening shift at the store, but not for a couple of hours. So she can grab a bowl of cereal at her computer and get in some time online before she has to leave for work.

At one time or another, someone questioned the safety of many of the chemicals Henry seemed to have used without a second thought. He always had an intense respect for authority figures. Sometimes Mary thought he had too much. He trusted the doctors to know how to keep him healthy, a trust that Mary believes was fatally misplaced. She has a lot of reading to do, but until she hears something back from Lawrence, there's no way she'd rather spend her time.

E.P.A. registrations don't seem to be of any help. Everything Henry used met the safety testing requirements. But then the E.P.A. might not have known what they were looking for any more than earlier genetics researchers did. The ingredients listed as inert are confusing. If they're inert, they shouldn't do anything. They look safe, but Mary's beginning to wonder if anything is safe.

Making her shift at work by less than a minute, Mary feels like she knows less than she did before. But she's determined to keep trying. She spots a little girl bouncing up to the register, followed by a beaming gray-haired woman. Mary realizes that the child is carrying a junior chemist set. She smiles at the adult holding out a credit card. "We don't see many kids that excited about science."

"Chemistry runs in our family," the customer explains. "I'm still working in my lab and teaching part-time at the university. So if my granddaughter stays with it when she's older, she'll be the fourth generation."

Mary leans across the counter and hands the girl a bag with her treasure before looking back at grandma. "What kind of chemistry do you teach?"

"The interaction of chemicals with the environment."

"Like the stuff used in yards?" Mary probes.

"Among many other things. Are you interested in ecology?" the customer queries.

Mary's hesitant to reveal too much in a public setting. "In a way. I have some questions about chemicals that might affect my family. Could I call you or come to see you?"

The grandmother chemist fishes around in her purse and pulls out a business card. She hands it to Mary. "Send me an email. We'll find a time."

Mary isn't sure what to say to the woman whose card identified her as Professor Sarah Greenspan, Ph.D. She sent Sarah a list of the products and chemicals she found in Henry's shed, hoping something would jump out to educated eyes. Sarah responded after a few hours with an invitation to visit. The shelves in Sarah's tiny office at the university, stuffed with references and journals, leave barely enough space for Sarah's desk and an extra chair.

Sarah waves Mary to the seat. "You probably already know that everything on your list was cleared for use by the E.P.A."

Mary's fingers twist in her lap. "I can't see my late husband, Henry, as having used anything that wasn't. He wanted our son, Chester, to have a safe place to play. He loved him very much."

Sarah leans toward Mary. "If I'm not prying, can I ask how your husband died?"

Mary swallows a rising lump of grief. "Cancer. He had cancer of the liver. The surgeons took the tumor out, but it had spread to his lungs and bones. He only lived for two years after his surgery. It was a hard time for our family. Chester swore that some evil corporation was giving people cancer so they could make money treating them. At the time, I thought that was his way of coping with Henry's death. But with all those chemicals, I'm wondering if something Henry used did make him sick. There are all those ads on TV from lawyers saying people got cancer from things that were supposed to be safe."

"I don't know about what lawyers claim," Sarah responds, "but science and testing techniques are always advancing. Unfortunately, there's so much legislative red tape tying up government procedures that it can take years to approve new protocols. But in my lab, we can move faster than that. We've been in the process of testing several of the components that are on your list, those formally designated as inert. What I've discovered hints at unanticipated interactions with D.N.A."

"Which components?" Mary demands.

Sarah drums her fingers on her desk. "I've yet to establish a high degree of confidence for what I've found. So at this moment, I'm not sure that having that data will do you any good."

Mary grabs the edge of Sarah's desk. "Look, I'm no scientist, and you don't know me. But I've gathered some information for a Milton Lawrence in California. Have you heard of him?"

"I've seen citations of his papers," Sarah responds. "None of them had a direct bearing on my work."

"If you can find a connection between his current research and yours, would you be willing to share your findings with him?" Mary demands.

"I'd be willing to correspond with him about it," Sarah allows.

Mary exhales the breath she hadn't realized she was holding. "That's better than nothing."

CHAPTER FOUR

Ever since she took Chester to his first psychologist, Mary's been pressing professionals, unsuccessfully, to come up with something useful. After meeting with Sarah Greenspan, she's more determined than ever to end that string of failures. If she has to put the key to working with Milton Lawrence under Sarah's nose, she will. Limiting her search for a chemical culprit to "inerts" won't help much. The women in her support group gave her, at most, product names. She'll have to find a common factor in all of them that piques Sarah's interests and correlates with Lawrence's findings.

The only person Mary trusts to help her is Lily. Unfortunately, Lily has no more chemical expertise than she does. They'll be bumbling along, but if they can get Sarah Greenspan and Milton Lawrence together, the academics can shift the hunt into high gear. Mary brews herself the strongest batch of iced tea she can manage. After settling down with a full glass, she starts throwing keywords at Google until she finds a group of inert compounds. They're on a list eligible for FIFRA pesticides - whatever those are. A bunch of them can be put in food. She figures those are the least dangerous. As she goes through the rest of them, she finds that most of the ones not permitted in edibles have names with benzoate or calcium in them. She's seen warnings on cereal boxes about something benzoate added to the packaging. Maybe that's a way of getting around putting it in the food. Could that be the clue she needs? The kids may not be allowed to eat whatever is affecting their already compromised genes. Still, they could get it all over themselves, rolling around in the grass. And what kids don't stick their hands in their mouths? It gives her a start she didn't have before and something she can share with Lily. For the first time since she talked to Doctor Lawrence, she feels like she's making at least a baby step forward.

Mary goes back to Henry's shed and starts taking pictures of labels. She wants to compare notes with Lily but immediately notices that only the active ingredients are listed on most bags and bottles. The rest make up more than half of the product. Why does the E.P.A. approve labels like that? How the hell can she look up something that's not there?

She'll have to research product by product and doubts that the chemical companies will make it easy. Now she really needs Lily. Maybe her friend has an idea where they can find more help. Mary hopes so. They'll need it.

Coffee slops over the side of Lily's mug as she sits across the kitchen table from Mary. Oh, my God! You mean the chemicals they put warnings about on those little cereal packages Evan used to love, in all that garden stuff, and it doesn't have to be listed on the label?"

"That's what I found out," Mary confirms. "It's politics or something. I don't understand how it works. But what poisoned our boys has to be in there somewhere, or supposedly harmless ingredients wouldn't be all over the E.P.A. documents. We'll just have to go over everything that got near the boys. The stuff not listed must be somewhere, but finding out where could take forever."

Lily wipes the table with a paper napkin before putting down her cup. "Maybe not. I met a lady at church who has multiple chemical sensitivities. She got them after a spill at the company she worked for. So now she has to stay outside the sanctuary at Easter because she's allergic to the flowers. I talked to her when she was watching from the narthex. She said all kinds of things put her in the hospital, so she's had to learn how to watch out for them. The college group helped her as a service project. So maybe we can get some of those kids to help us out."

Half out of her seat, Mary leans across the table. "Do you know any of them?"

Biting her bottom lip, Lily shakes her head. "No, but the church secretary will have a roster. She'll be in tomorrow morning. I can call and ask her."

The eyes in 19-year-old Kelly Juno's face are solemn with experience beyond her years. "It's all about money," she explains. "The chemical companies claim their formulations as trade secrets, so they don't have to put the supposedly inert ingredients on the label. It's garbage! To be a trade secret, those components would have to do something, and they do. But this way, consumers can't ask too many questions. Their lobbyists write the laws, so the E.P.A. lets the industry get away with it."

What's left of Mary's fingernails dig into her palms. "So if the chemical companies can hide what's in their products, how do we find out?"

"There are ways. Some states have their own registration requirements. Sometimes we can dig out the information that way. Some organizations also file Freedom of Information Act requests, but that can take a while, and the courts can turn them down. The fastest thing is to request safety data sheets. Unfortunately, manufacturers often ask you for your company's name and contact information before you can get them. Still, if you have friends, it's not hard."

"Who has that kind of friends?" Mary wonders.

"I do," Kelly announces. "Two of my uncles have farms. They've switched over to growing organics because of what they learned about some of the pesticides. But they don't mind me using them as fronts to get information. Actually, they love it."

Mary only takes a second to consider why she's opening a fat envelope of safety data sheets like a kid tears open wrappings on Christmas morning. Despite the number of sheets of paper, it contains few complete documents. In those, only a couple of sections matter, the ones identifying the components of a product and the supposed health risks involved.

Kelly already warned her that regarding the list of health risks as complete is like believing a politician's speech. Sometimes things are left out, and even if they aren't, they're cast in the best possible light. The manufacturers have an even more effective insurance policy than that. They merely claim that information is unknown or unavailable. Of course, the reason it's unavailable is that they lobbied against testing for it or refused to pay the freight. Still, even with all that, lucky eyes can find a nugget or two buried in the gravel of meaningless data.

Of the four data sheets stuffed into the envelope, three list their inert ingredients as having no known hazards. That's useless. The fourth is a bit more comprehensive but only discloses irritation to the respiratory system. Not much help there either. Mary already stumbled on articles saying that kids exposed to herbicides suffered more respiratory infections. If the crap affects the kids' lungs, they must inhale it or something. Mary marks the information with an orange highlighter and tucks the data sheet into a bright red accordion file. The authors didn't provide any mechanism, but it's a start. With an extra-wide marker, she labels her file "SUSPECTS."

Lily's I.D. appears on Mary's chiming cellphone. "Did they come?" she asks as soon as Mary accepts the call.

"Yeah, but only one with anything we can use. It's the sheet for 'Perfect Lawn.'"

"I think our landscaping service used that," Lily recalls. The TV commercials have that silly mascot. I remember seeing a picture of it on the bag."

"Right. It's on one of the bags in Henry's shed, too. We'll have to check if the kids of the other members of the group had contact with that weed killer, but I want to wait until we have a longer list. If we have to keep asking about stuff they've never heard of, more of them could start ducking out of meetings. I'm crossing my fingers that more sheets come in soon."

"I'm putting it on my prayer list," Lily responds.

"I'll take all the help we can get." Mary agrees. "But I don't see anything on the data sheets about what Doctor Lawrence is studying. The chemical companies may not know if a component has any effects like that."

Lily sniffs. "Or they might be like the tobacco companies who knew smoking caused cancer and covered it up. After everything we've seen them do to hide what they put in their products, we can't trust them for a second."

"You're right," Mary agrees. "We can't."

CHAPTER FIVE

FOUR MONTHS LATER

The circle of chairs in the church basement is smaller, but so is the questionnaire Mary hands out. It took her and Lily all this time to come up with less than a page. But between the two of them, they think they've found the most likely suspects. At least they hope so. If they get matches from the group, they will have something solid to take to Sarah Greenspan. While the other parents decide whether to mark a box or not, Mary and Lily alternate between crossing their fingers and praying.

"Everyone checked off either Weed-O, Broad-B-Gone, or Perfect Lawn," Lily notes as she and Mary tally the group's answers. So what do they have in common?"

Mary studies her lists. "Not the same chemical, but half a chemical. They both have benzoates like the cereal box packaging. Weed-O and Perfect Lawn have calcium benzoate, and Broad-B-Gone has sodium benzoate."

"That's got to be close enough, right?" Lily pulls out her phone. "I'm going to call Kelly. She should know."

Sarah Greenspan studies the write-up Kelly helped Mary craft. "I've run up against benzoates before. They've been around a long time. But I've never looked at their epigenetic implications. I believe that at this point, it makes sense for me to contact Doctor Lawrence. I'll arrange a conference and get back to you."

"How soon?" Mary presses.

"As soon as I can, Ms. Taxtrum. Look, you've put a lot of work and passion into this. But there is only so much time and more to the point, so much research funding. If I can work out a way to collaborate with Doctor Lawrence, I will. But I'm not making any promises I can't keep. I hope you understand."

Mary forces a breath into her lungs. "I understand, Doctor Greenspan. Over the years, a lot of 'experts' made promises to me about my son, Chester. They didn't keep any of them. Just let me know what's going on, OK?"

"That," Greenspan assures her, "I can promise."

Recognizing a California area code, Mary hurriedly accepts a call. Lawrence's enthusiasm is evident as it pours through the speaker. "Ms. Taxtrum, I've just had a fascinating conversation with Doctor Greenspan. I'm impressed by the data you gathered, very impressed. But I was wondering if it might be possible for you to take your research a step further."

"What step?" Mary queries.

"We have the D.N.A. sequences you acquired, but we need more from individuals displaying the behaviors you described and also from close relatives. Would it be possible for you to help us obtain them? Doctor Greenspan can make sure they are properly gathered if you can direct her to the subjects contributing to your data."

Air whistles through Mary's lips. "Membership in my group is confidential. I can't just give names to Doctor Greenspan without permission. I can get the parents to agree, at least some of them. But you understand how our children behave. They don't believe there's anything wrong with them. What can we tell them?"

"I'll have to leave that to you," Lawrence admits. "Think about it and let me know."

Lily stares at her iced tea as if the stray bits of leaves floating in it would suddenly form an answer. "Mary, what are we going to do? We have enough problems with the parents in the group. How are we going to convince the kids?"

Mary's glass clatters as she vigorously stirs in already dissolved sugar. "Maybe we can use the way they are instead of trying to fight it."

Lily crushes a paper napkin in her fist. "How?"

"When Chester was little, I tried to get him to do what I wanted by making it fit in with whatever he believed. I still used Santa Claus to motivate him when he was 12! Maybe we can tell the kids that they're going to prove that how they think is a step up from ordinary people. I know Chester believes anyone who disagrees with him is an idiot."

"So does Evan," Lily agrees. "It could work."

Mary drops her spoon on the table. "I hope so."

The small gathering in a university lab looks smug and expectant as Doctor Greenspan's graduate student swabs the insides of their cheeks. They've all been told they've been chosen to participate in a study because of their clear thinking. The student also gives them a brief questionnaire to fill out regarding their belief systems and political bents. The questionnaires aren't quite a sham. Doctor Laurence told Mary they'd be useful.

Of course, she and Lily can't show their faces. Most of the kids of the parents in the group have seen them at one time or another. But Greenspan's students are strangers and seemingly admiring ones. The white-coated girl gathering samples plays her part well.

Seven men and one woman volunteered to be tested. Despite the absence of any pain, they all, including the woman, Miranda, seem to be competing to see who can be the most macho about being swabbed. Miranda wins in her own opinion, but all the individuals tested credit superiority to themselves. They would be funny if their behavior didn't cause so much misery to their families.

The pizza Mary arranged to have delivered for the participants almost triggers a fight. Attempting to keep everyone happy, she ordered thick and thin crusts. Unfortunately, members of the group decided that preferences other than their own were stupid. Greenspan's students manage to distract them by dissing veggie pizza, which none of them can stand.

After the session, Mary comes out of hiding to overnight the precious samples to a lab at the university where Doctor Lawrence conducts his research. She'd love to put her feet up with a glass of wine but has to make her shift at the toy store.

Mary uses the little time she has before going to work to check the local paper. She's one of the few people she knows who still gets a print edition. Online articles are more current but often posted too quickly. They can be full of errors that spread through social media before they can be corrected.

Messed up information like that seems to find Chester with lightning speed. He'll take a crazy idea to heart, and once he does, there's no way to change his mind. That's what got him in trouble. He thought he was confronting evil when he was chasing a lie. But he couldn't see the truth in front of his face. Even after being arrested for what he did, he still believes it was the right thing.

For a long time, Mary blamed herself for Chester's stubbornness. That demon still claws at her in the middle of the night. Finding out that there's a physical reason, something interacting with his genes, will make all the difference. At least, she hopes it will.

An article about her congressman, Ray Schiller, catches her eye while wrenching her gut. She thinks he's a useless fool and didn't vote for him. But Chester loves him and hangs on his every word. Schiller's growing in popularity and number of followers, including the kids of other support group members. They show up, cheering every time he makes an appearance.

Mary shivers at the latest reporting. Chester is getting dangerous enough on his own. A mob of Chester's ready to do the bidding of a clueless politician could make for disaster. So far, Schiller's band of local supporters is small, but according to the paper, he may be running for the Senate. God only knows what kind of garbage will come out of him if he needs to pull in voters statewide - and what Schiller's followers, like Chester, will take as gospel.

CHAPTER SIX

Rory Montrose carefully estimates the size of the crowd surrounding the podium where Ray Schiller is making his speech. He figures Ray's attracted 200 followers at most, but they're enthusiastic and loud. As long as the cameraman doesn't use too wide an angle, the group should look impressive on video.

In the front row, the young people listen with rapt attention to Ray's B.S., whistling, applauding, and repeating his lame chants. Whatever works. Before they go, Rory will make sure they're signed up as volunteers. Kids like them are as crazy as Ray acts. They'll stand in hot sun or pouring rain just to pass on his message that the country is in trouble and he's the only one who can save it.

Ray's boogie man, boogie woman, really, is Senator Nathalie Wellstone. To hear Ray tell it, she's a demon incarnate, ready to confiscate their guns and sell children as sex slaves. Never mind that Nathalie is a grandmother who's spent decades in public service. Ray's spun his horrifying tales so often that Rory thinks the pol is actually starting to believe them. That makes him even more convincing.

That afternoon, Ray's smears are coming hot and fast: "Nathalie Wellstone is a secret pedophile who ships children to the Middle East in chains. Nathalie Wellstone had an affair with the president and is controlling him through blackmail. Nathalie Wellstone releases classified material to enemy countries." Some of Ray's claims are his greatest hits. Others he's making up on the spot.

Part of the crowd starts drifting away, shaking their heads. But the disciples Rory spotted in the front row are riveted, working themselves into a frenzy as they shout, "Bury the Wellstone!" Before they leave, they'll be fully primed to do Ray's bidding. And Rory will find lots for them to do. They will be the spearhead of the army that will bring Ray to power. And Rory will be behind the throne, out of the line of fire, whispering in Ray's ear.

Finally, back in his home state, Chester's found the man he's been seeking, the savior who can turn the country around. Ray sees the truth the way Chester does, and the young man will do anything for his idol. Barely out of jail, Chester's just getting on his feet. He doesn't have much in the way of money, but he'll give Ray every minute he can spare. The cause is too important to do anything less.

Ray tips back his beer, downing half the bottle. "Who's that new volunteer you picked up, the one from the front row at the rally?"

Rory sips his pale ale. "You couldn't miss him, could you? His name is Chester Taxtrum. He's a true believer, the one who bought the story about the pedophilia ring and went in waving a gun. He still buys it, and he's inhaling every word you say. He has friends who swallow it, too. I put him to work recruiting them. The girl who was standing near him, Miranda, will be working on pulling in other ladies. She's as into it as Chester is."

"They're not screwing each other, are they?" Ray demands. "We don't need that kind of complication in the campaign."

Rory shakes his head. "Nah! You've got all of their attention. But we can use both of them for mixed target groups."

"Keep an eye on them and whoever they pull in," Ray advises. "Dedicated is great, but we don't need batshit until we gain more momentum. One bad story originating from our campaign can set us back weeks or months."

"I'll take care of it," Rory promises.

A saucer clatters beneath Lily's cup. "I didn't think Evan could get much crazier, but now he's following that nutcase, Schiller. He's out in front of Walmart today, trying to get the customers to sign some kind of petition to indict Nathalie Wellstone. That poor woman helped get funding for the services he's used for most of his life, and now Schiller's convinced him that she's possessed by demons."

Closing her eyes, Mary nods. "I know. Chester's following that lunatic too. But anything I say against that madman just makes him more determined. We've got to support Nathalie Wellstone. There's no other way to stop Schiller."

Lily pushes her coffee away. "If we do that, our kids are going to hate us."

Mary rakes back her graying hair. "If we don't, Schiller will lead our boys and a lot of others straight into hell. I saw Wellstone's people working on opening an office right near the toy store where I work. I'm going to stop in there before my shift starts and find out if there's anything I can do to help. Can you come with me?"

Lily's teeth dig into her bottom lip. "I can't, Mary, not now. Doctor Lawrence doesn't know what's going to happen with our kids. Maybe the gene that got turned off can turn on again, and I can talk some sense into Evan. Sometimes it seems like he's listening, at least a little. I can't risk completely losing him. I'm sorry."

Driven by habit, Mary clears away the coffee cups. "I understand. If I thought there was any other way I could drag Chester back into reality, I wouldn't bother with a political campaign. But the Chester I knew the first years of his life, before whatever happened to change him, is gone. I can't even see a sign of him anymore. If he stays with Schiller, he'll feed on every crackpot idea that comes out of that maniac's mouth. I've got to do everything I can to stop that man. Nathalie Wellstone could be the only way.

Lily wraps trembling arms around her friend. "Good luck."

Two hours before her shift at work begins, Mary wanders into the storefront becoming Nathalie Wellstone Headquarters. She'd hoped to see a hive of activity but only finds one person at a computer and another painting a wall. Mentally flipping a coin, Mary approaches the woman at the computer. "I want to sign up to volunteer."

Liz Farnsworth pops up from her slightly wobbly desk chair. "God bless you! Do you have any experience with a political campaign?"

"I painted signs once when I was twelve, but not really." Mary confides.

Liz's hand sweeps through the air as if flicking away bad thoughts. "Never mind. We can always use an extra pair of hands. Right now, we could use about ten extra pairs of hands. Can you type?"

Mary considers the hunt and peck that picked up speed with her research. "More or less."

"Good enough," Liz enthuses, pointing to a clipboard full of petitions at an empty workstation. "We need to get the names and contact information off those and into our database so we can reach the people in favor of Nathalie's policies. It's pretty easy. You just fill them in and hit enter. But some of Schiller's followers have been trying to pull numbers on us by putting in phony information. Before you enter anything, google the names and see if those people are real. Otherwise, we'll be wasting a lot of time and money trying to reach them, which is just what Schiller wants. That, pardon my French, asshole's, people will do anything to win. Can you start now?"

Mary glances at her watch. "I'm due at work at the Toy Emporium at six, but I can help until then."

Liz slaps her palm against a table. "Sold! Let's get you started!"

CHAPTER SEVEN

Mary stands and applauds with the rest of the volunteers and staff as Nathalie Wellstone enters her storefront headquarters. Laugh lines fan from the senator's eyes as she smiles at her crew. "You are the soul of my campaign, the soul of this country. I don't have to tell you that our job is getting harder every day. Ray Schilling is, to put it bluntly, a liar, but a very skillful one. He's mastered the art of repetition. The more often the voters hear something, the more strongly they tend to believe it.

"Right now, his lies are drowning out our truths. We can't allow that to go on. I need all of you, and every minute, every second you can give me. But more than that, I need your friends, your neighbors, your families. Talk to them. Make them understand that Ray Schiller's way means turning our backs on everything that made this country great. His message is insidious. He preaches that by denying the knowledge we and our allies fought so hard to gain, this country can return to happier, more secure days. But the picture he paints is of times that never existed.

"Some of you are old enough to remember when we all knew someone in braces from polio. The numbers on people's arms weren't from the local tattoo parlor. Our fellow citizens asking merely for equal treatment were met with clubs and fire hoses. Schiller would have us return to the black hole of ignorance and fear. We are better than that. We are stronger than that. And by holding on to what we know is right, we will keep this country walking in the light. We will have to be louder and more determined than Schiller, but I know we can do it. I feel it in every bone in my body. Do you feel it too?"

Mary finds herself clapping harder than she can ever remember slamming her hands together as cheers and whistles rebound from the walls. Nathalie stretches out her arms, clapping back at her supporters. "You're all incredible. And I have a surprise for you. Our campaign has joined forces with the Clean Food Project. As you may know, supported by academic research, the organization explores the long-ranging effects of chemicals on our food supply and health. One of its targets is a multinational that is supporting Schiller. They're going to be holding a tasting of some incredible and pesticide-free street food. And we're invited. We're also inviting this neighborhood and neighborhoods around the state to experience what we can enjoy when we work with environmental science instead of denying it. So let's have some fun."

To Ray Schiller, the Low-Dunn conference room is like a flashback to the '60s, or at least what he's seen on old '60s television shows. The only woman present is pouring coffee. Her skirt is short, and her hair is piled high. She only speaks when asked a question and takes notes of what every speaker says. Some of the executives even have ashtrays at their places. Ray can't remember the last time he saw one anywhere else. The smoke is irritating his throat, but he isn't about to object. Low-Dunn is pouring millions of dollars into a PAC supporting his campaign, and he can't afford to interrupt the flow.

CEO Monteith Metzger stubs out his cigarette. "Mr. Schiller, our largest concern is Nathalie Wellstone's collaboration with environmental activists. As you know, they consider our products, unjustly, of course, as having adverse effects on health. They've also accused us of twisting the arms of farmers to use our herbicide-resistant seed. We need an advocate in the Senate to steer rulemaking legislation in the right direction. We trust that you understand our needs."

Ray takes a sip of water to suppress a cough. "Of course, Mr. Metzger. Low-Dunn's contribution to the economy of this country is undeniable. If I'm elected to the Senate, you can count on my support."

"Then," Metzger asserts, "We'll make sure you're elected."

"We have a problem," Nathalie Wellstone admits to Liz Farnsworth over early-morning coffee at campaign headquarters. "A PAC supporting Schiller just got a massive infusion of cash. From what I've been able to find out, the money came from Low-Dunn."

"So they're banking on Schiller to be their front man to fight pesticide regulation," Liz infers.

"That's what I make of it," Nathalie agrees. "Our environmental coalition doesn't have anyone with nearly that kind of resources to back it."

"It doesn't matter," Liz insists. "We're going to the small donors. None of them can give that much, but there are a lot of them. I met with the Gray-Haired Warriors yesterday. It's a bunch of grandmothers and even a few grandfathers who want to make sure their grandchildren can drink the water and eat the food on this planet. The young people are getting fired up too. They don't want to end up living in some poisonous hell-hole. Their moms don't want them to, either."

"Then we need to put together a group to spread the message that big corporations intend to rob the children of their future in exchange for a quick buck," Nathalie declares.

"That's not just a message; it's the truth," Liz points out.
Nathalie sighs. "Unfortunately, that doesn't make it any easier to convince people to believe it.

Liz grabs the karaoke microphone she uses to boost her voice in Nathalie's headquarters. "I need everyone's attention. Some of you may have noticed the new ads running against Nathalie, saying that the environmental regulations she champions will destroy the country's agriculture industry. We all know that claim is false. In fact, a great many farmers who are experiencing the effects of climate change support Nathalie's efforts.

"Unless you read the small print very quickly, it's impossible to tell that those ads are funded by a political action committee. That PAC is, in turn, supported by Low-Dunn, a chemical manufacturer. One of its most lucrative products is an herbicide Nathalie is attempting to get the E.P.A. to ban. If you're not familiar with the issues involved, read the handout in Nathalie's campaign literature.

"Most likely, as a result of those ads, Nathalie is beginning to slip in the polls. We can't let that happen. Nathalie doesn't have any industrial giants behind her, for good reason. She's there for us, ordinary people just fighting for a better world for our children and grandchildren. That means that instead of the big donations supporting Schiller, we'll need to call on Nathalie's supporters for a lot of little ones.

"Many of you will hate what I'm going to be asking you to do. I know I hate doing it. But we have to call people and knock on doors. We'll tell them heart to heart why we support Nathalie and need their help, even if it's just a few dollars. I'm going to be handing out assignment sheets. If you can't make calls from here, you can make them from home. Meet with your friends, your family, members of your religious organizations, anyone you can. If we're going to give our kids a future, it's all hands on deck. Can I hear a yes?"

Before she knows what she's doing, Mary shouts her answer.

As Nathalie's volunteers return to work with renewed enthusiasm, Mary approaches Liz. "There's something about Low-Dunn that Nathalie might want to know."

CHAPTER EIGHT

Are you telling me that one of Low-Dunn's products makes people act like Schiller followers?" Liz demands.

"I'm saying that I'm part of a group involved with research into what we've been calling 'the believe gene.' My son Chester, and others like him, accept all kinds of crazy stuff, including Schiller's conspiracy theories. But it's complicated," Mary adds. "It has to do with a drug I and the other mothers took when we were pregnant that makes a gene vulnerable to something called epigenetics. If Nathalie wants to find out about it, I can put her in touch with Doctor Milton Lawrence in California and Doctor Sarah Greenspan here. They can explain the whole thing a lot better than I can."

"Give me Lawrence and Greenspan's contact information," Liz instructs. "I'll pass it and what you said on to Nathalie. But I don't know if she'll want to do anything about it. She has a hell of a lot on her plate."

Mary nods. "I understand. But if she's up against Low-Dunn, she should know as much as possible."

"I agree with you on that," Liz acknowledges.

"We can't cite research that hasn't been peer-reviewed or even published," Nathalie insists in a late-night meeting with Liz. "That would make us no better than Schiller."

"I get that," Liz responds. "But I believe that Mary Taxtrum shared that information with me because it's something she wanted us to understand, not announce to the general public. If some or all of Schiller's followers are "hardwired," so to speak, to believe his crap, there may be nothing we can do to change their minds. We'll have to work around them and present our evidence to people capable of accepting it."

Nathalie slowly nods. "Meaning we wouldn't waste time and energy fighting battles we can't win. We'd have to make our case to voters who need more information, not an argument. We can do that, but we'd need to get some surrogates with unassailable credentials on board. That isn't easy. A lot of scientists prefer to remain apolitical and stick to their work."

"If they try to do that under Schiller and his gang, they may find they have no work to stick to," Liz points out.

"Unfortunately true," Nathalie agrees. "We may have some difficult but essential recruiting to do."

Sarah Greenspan never expected a call, let alone a visit, from Nathalie Wellstone. Politicians make noises about science, for and against, all the time, and Ray Schiller is particularly obnoxious in his anti-science rhetoric. But apparently, his opponent is interested in more than making speeches. "Senator, if I understood Ms. Farnsworth correctly, you've received information from Mary Taxtrum."

"Mary Taxtrum is a volunteer on my campaign. When she realized that Low-Dunn supports Ray Schiller, she thought some research you and she are involved in might be relevant. Mary mentioned a Low-Dunn product having an influence on disciples of demagogues like Schiller. It sounded a little far-fetched to me, but I checked out your reputation. Your record is solid. So tell me, Doctor Greenspan, is there anything to what Mary Taxtrum said?"

Sarah folds her hands on the desk in front of her. "Mary Taxtrum told you the truth, as much as we know of it, which isn't a lot. We're dealing with a very small sample. So far, the D.N.A. analysis has supported the interaction of a Low-Dunn product with the effects of a drug taken by the affected cohort's mothers during pregnancy. There is no control group and no cohort with similar behaviors but without the epigenetic effects. In addition to that, the component in the Low-Dunn product we theorize to have triggered the chromosomal changes is generally classed as inert in that application. At this point in our research, we can't claim results that any responsible journal would publish."

"But...," Nathalie prompts.

"We have zero evidence counter to our theory. In a study like this, we would expect outliers, contradictory results. As yet, we have seen none. There is a strong possibility that a Low-Dunn product has produced a genetically distinct group of young people that, among other characteristics, support the company's goals. We suspect this was entirely coincidental, but a positive outcome for Low-Dunn and those with politics like Ray Schiller."

"So, how can I help you?" Nathalie inquires.

"We could use government support to expand our research," Sarah suggests. "We won't get that under an administration that implements

Schiller's policies. Fight like hell to keep your seat, Senator Wellstone. Further study is the only way we'll get to the truth."

Nathalie pushes out of her chair, extending her hand. "Doctor Greenspan, I intend to do exactly that."

"We may have a problem," Rory suggests to Schiller. "Wellstone is going upstate to where all the organic farms are. They already back all her natural foods garbage. But she's pushing the point that herbicides do more than poison harmless plants and insects. They're bad for the health of children. She dug up some research showing that kids around grass dosed with herbicides get more respiratory infections."

Schiller shrugs. "Kids in neighborhoods full of roaches get more asthma. No one cares. No one who matters, anyway."

"That's the thing, Ray. The people who support those farms do matter," Rory insists. "They go to four-star restaurants and shop in upscale markets. They have money and the wherewithal to make the media pay attention."

"Low-Dunn knows how to fight them. They've been doing it for years." Schiller argues.

"But Nathalie has young supporters who weren't around years ago. They don't like the legacy their parents and corporations like Low-Dunn have dumped on them, and they're willing to fight back."

"We have our own young army," Ray retorts. "If those candy-ass kids want a battle, they'll get one, a bigger one than they bargained for."

"Are you talking about taking the Alpha Wolves up on their offer?" Rory inquires. "I didn't think you wanted anything to do with biker gangs."

"It turns out we have a common enemy," Ray explains. "The bikers don't care much about the other issues, but Wellstone championed helmet laws, and they want to be free to get their brains bashed in."

"So, what are the Wolves going to do for us?" Rory asks.

"Mostly provide the fear factor. They'll be showing up at Wellstone's rallies, obstructing access, gunning their engines so the crowd can't hear the speeches - that kind of thing. They'll be drowning out her message while ours stays loud and clear."

Rory nods. "Smooth strategy, Boss."

Ray winks. "Those boys on their hogs will put Nathalie's supporters on the run."

Mary glances nervously over her shoulder. She could barely make it to Nathalie's rally, with motorcycles blocking most of the entrances into the parking lot. But if the bikers wanted to discourage Nathalie's followers, they failed. The crowd is a little smaller than usual but still very enthusiastic. And Mary and the other campaign workers are getting signature after signature on petitions to protect waterways from chemical runoff.

Some of Low-Dunn's fertilizers are heavy-duty contributors to water pollution. The corporation isn't going to like Nathalie's latest crusade at all. That's fine with Mary. She's come to the conclusion that if Low-Dunn thinks something is a good idea; she'll probably be against it.

She hasn't heard much from Doctor Lawrence about how his research is coming along, but he told her it would be a while before he got back to her. If waiting is what it takes to get proof of what happened to Chester and the others like him, she'll wait as long as it takes. And in the meantime, she'll work as hard as she can to make sure Low-Dunn's errand boy doesn't make it to the Senate. The corporation already has too much influence on the government. She's not about to let them grab any more.

CHAPTER NINE

Chester envies the Alpha Wolves. He'd love to ride a motorcycle, but he can barely afford to keep his car running on the pitiful wages he earns as a convicted felon. It's not fair. He did the right thing, the moral thing, and got punished for it. He's free now, but if corrupt politicians like Nathalie Wellstone stay in office, he'll keep getting screwed. He can't do the bikers' job, but he can still help Ray Schiller rescue the country.

Today, he's knocking on doors to tell voters what a menace to democracy Nathalie Wellstone is, but he's not having a lot of luck. If the citizens in this neighborhood open their doors at all, they tell him that they think that Wellstone is doing a good job. A couple of them even told him how the senator helped them out personally. They must have been either liars or crazy. Their stories couldn't have been true.

He only has a few more blocks to cover before he can go to the rally that night. He'll have a great time. Rory is letting some of the volunteers come backstage to meet the Schiller supporters playing the music. Schiller hasn't got some of the big names that Wellstone has. Chester snorts in disgust. So many bands are left-wing radicals. He doesn't know why people even go to their concerts. The patriotic groups supporting Schiller are still good and get the crowd going, so Schiller can deliver his message. That's what matters, getting the truth out there, whatever it takes.

Nathalie and Liz watch the live feed of the Schiller rally on YouTube. "He's got the cameras placed to make the crowd look a lot bigger than it is," Liz notes. "And the band is strictly D-list."

"A-list musicians attract people to our rallies but don't necessarily get us votes," Nathalie points out. "How's the canvassing going?"

"Not good. Whenever the Schiller campaign finds out our people are working an area, he sends in the Alpha Wolves to buzz the streets and chase potential voters behind locked doors. Some of our volunteers are also too afraid to work with the bikers around."

"That strategy may be a double-edged sword for Schiller," Nathalie suggests. "The Wolves can't force a choice in the privacy of the voting booth. Who is likely to check the box for someone whose minions spread terror in their neighborhood? Arrange for a phone and online poll. Find out how likely voters are reacting. We may be able to turn Schiller's tactics to our advantage."

"I'll get right on it," Liz pledges.

Mary has never liked making phone calls. She doesn't mind answering them or talking to people in person, but her stomach tightens every time she punches in a number. Yet somehow, she finds herself on a phone bank working for Nathalie. She's taking a poll, but when she says so, most people don't believe her. She's had enough telemarketers call her claiming to take a poll before trying to sell her something or asking for a contribution, to understand that reaction. Still, she digs in. Liz said Nathalie needs the information. That's enough to keep Mary going.

So far, the responses she's getting from people actually willing to talk to her aren't bad. Most of them seem to honestly want a clean environment. Many of the ones who have heard Schiller find him obnoxious, although a few think he's funny. Some of the responders admit to being scared of the Alpha Wolves, but they also resent being intimidated. That should be good for Nathalie. All in all, when Mary finishes her shift, she feels good about what she heard. Next time she'll be a little less nervous.

With the air in the Low-Dunn conference room thick with smoke, Grover Norliss, the front man for Schiller's PAC, attempts to justify requesting more funds. "You have to admit, Ray's been doing an excellent job for you. He's got almost a third of the state believing that environmentalists are naive boobs who are going to wreck the economy and drive the country into recession."

"Exactly the attitude we're attempting to promote, but almost a third isn't nearly enough. Your boss has to win big," Monteith Metzger insists. "As the new boy on the block in the Senate, he'll need to secure the committee assignments to steer legislation in the right direction. He'll also need to whisper in the right ears to get the presidential appointments we want - EPA, Interior, USDA, and HHS. We need the tree-huggers and bleeding hearts out."

"Mr. Metzger, that is precisely the point I wanted to make," Grover claims. "Schiller doesn't just need a win. He needs an overwhelming mandate, and that takes money, a lot of it. But I promise you, your investment now will pay off big time as soon as Ray Schiller replaces Nathalie Wellstone in the Senate."

"It better," Metzger warns. "Schiller does not want to see a future without our support, and he can take that to the bank."

Liz hands Nathalie an oversized mug of coffee. "Here, you're going to need this, and you might want to put something stronger in it. I just heard that Low-Dunn is pouring another ten million into Schiller's PAC."

"You're right," Nathalie agrees. "I could use something stronger. How are we going to raise that kind of money?"

"I'm not sure we have to," Liz responds. "I have an idea, but it's going to take some doing. We know from our polls that when people are told, or better yet shown, what Schiller is putting out there, they think it's sickening. The problem is, most people don't know."

"And if they don't know, they won't care enough to vote against him," Nathalie realizes. "But again, we're up against the money. We need ads to get the message across, and air time costs."

"Unless we use exactly what he says against him," Liz counters. "We can get raw footage of his rallies, shot on cell phones. Then we'll organize every one of our people to put the video out on social media with a simple message: 'Is this who you want running your country?' It won't cost a dime. But the Alpha Wolves could be dangerous. Our observers will have to make sure they don't get caught. And we'll have to be upfront that it might be dangerous."

"Of course, we'll be upfront," Nathalie exclaims. "That's the point, isn't it, that Schiller is the liar fooling all those people into buying his crap? No one should step up who isn't willing to take the risk. But I have faith. Our people know what Schiller is and what the stakes are if he wins this election."

Mary had her doubts if she could even stomach a Schiller rally, but she seems to fit in with some of the attendees. Schiller attracts middle-aged blue-collar voters who are hoping for better days. That describes Mary as well as anyone. She just doesn't expect Schiller to turn things around. If anything, he'll make them worse.

Mary pulls out her phone as Schiller begins his speech. She's going to try to record the worst of it. She's just managed to capture some video of Schiller claiming that environmentalists will tank the economy when she spots Chester coming her way. She doesn't know if he's seen her, but she's not about to find out. She shoves her phone in her pocket and starts to leave, but Chester blocks her way.

Mary's son opens his arms for a hug. "You finally accepted the truth! I'm so happy for you, Mom. Maybe we can work for Schiller together to get this country on the right path."

"I really just came to find out what he has to say," Mary responds, trying her best not to completely lie to her son.

Chester grins. "That's all right. Almost everyone starts that way. As soon as Ray's finished spreading the word, I can introduce you to the right people to get you into the campaign."

With no idea what else to do, Mary agrees.

CHAPTER TEN

"Are you telling me that Mary Taxtrum is embedded with the Schiller campaign?" Nathalie demands.

"I don't know how deep into the campaign she is," Liz clarifies. "But from what she told me, once her son spotted her at a rally, she had to play along with his conclusion that she'd become a Schiller supporter. They haven't got her doing anything important yet, just organizing campaign merchandise. I guess her son told the staff that Mary's in retail. But she'll be at the rallies now, and no one will think twice about her taking video. We'll just have to make sure nothing in what we post will lead back to her. I have our IT guy looking into any scrubbing we'll need to do. He's a volunteer. He'll do it for free."

"Sounds like we got lucky," Nathalie remarks, "but are you sure Mary can pull off her masquerade?"

"No," Liz admits. "Neither is she. But she's going to do her damnedest to try."

The stench of tobacco smoke reaches Mary's nose before she spots the man in a suit coming down the aisle to the back office of Schiller headquarters. In the last ten years, she hasn't met too many people who reek like that. With spaces where smoking is allowed growing fewer and fewer, smokers rarely get the chance to light up. And even when they can, cigarettes are damned expensive. She doubts the cost would bother that guy, not from the fit of his suit. Hand tailoring isn't cheap. With the visitor's unpleasant aura still hanging in the air, Mary decides to slip outside for a moment. A shiny gas guzzler is parked at the curb. A car like that would fit with the smoker's suit. She notices a sticker on the back window and shifts her position to grab a look. It's a logo, crossed out crabgrass with a super-imposed "L.D." She's seen it before on the bags from Henry's shed. The "L.D." stands for Low-Dunn. Those bastards would tie-up with Schiller!"

"Is Mary sure she saw someone from Low-Dunn at Schiller headquarters?" Nathalie questions.

"She's sure she saw someone with a Low-Dunn sticker on his car," Liz corrects, "but close enough."

"Maybe," Nathalie considers. "Low-Dunn can legally give all the money it wants to a PAC, but a PAC coordinating with a campaign is illegal. We'd have to be sure before trying to do anything with the information. Tell Mary to keep at it. Pump up her confidence as much as you can. She has no idea how important this information could be to the campaign."

"Being able to nail Low-Dunn is probably even more important to her," Liz points out. "Schiller is bad enough. But she sees Low-Dunn as responsible for turning her sweet little boy into a conspiracy freak. That's about as much motivation as anyone could have."

"As long as her enthusiasm doesn't make her careless. If Schiller figures out she's a plant, God only knows what could happen, but nothing good," Nathalie worries.

"I've warned her, but I'll do it again," Liz promises.

As soon as Mary recognizes the visitor from Low-Dunn, she reaches for her cellphone. She wants to get a picture of him, but Liz urged her to be careful - not that she needed urging. She can only get him in profile without being noticed, but she hopes it's enough. This time he's meeting with Rory, the highest-ranking person in the campaign, except for Schiller himself. Whatever they're talking about must be important.

Surveying the layout, Mary realizes that the ladies' room shares a wall with the back office. From a stall, she might be able to hear part of the conversation or even record it. No one will be looking at her or wondering what she's doing in there. And her stomach is beginning to clench. She does have to go.

Mary slips her phone back into her pocket before leaving the ladies' room. She didn't understand a lot of what she heard, but she recorded as much as she could. Even if she can't figure out what it means, there's a good chance that Liz or even Nathalie can.

She doesn't dare to do anything that might attract attention. Mary finishes her task of updating shirt and hat inventories. The job isn't a lot different from some of what she was doing for Nathalie, and she's tempted to screw it up. But if she does, she could lose her position as a Schiller volunteer. As long as she can help Nathalie by staying with Schiller, Mary's not about to take any chances. The time drags, but finally, she's able to get out and take what she has to Wellstone headquarters.

"Do we know who those men are?" Nathalie asks, listening intensely to the conversation Mary caught on her phone.

"We can confirm that one voice is Rory Montrose, Schiller's campaign manager. He's all over the media. We don't know about the second one, other than Mary's suspicion that he works for Low-Dunn," Liz explains. "But from their discussion, it's obvious that he is associated with Low-Dunn's PAC supporting Schiller. That alone should nail both Low-Dunn and Schiller for violation of campaign finance law."

"Only if we can make a definitive identification of that voice," Nathalie responds. "Let's use our connection with the university. It must have an audio lab or something that can nail an I.D."

Liz nods enthusiastically. "That's a good idea. I'll put someone on it."

"Do it yourself, Liz," Nathalie instructs. "We can't afford for anything about this recording to leak out."

"Right," Liz agrees.

Audio-engineering instructor Laughlin looks up at Liz from her computer and attached oscilloscope. "I don't usually have anything to do with politics, but the powers-that-be told me it would give me a leg up on renewing my contract if I helped you out. And this is an interesting project. I might even get a paper out of it. So let me make sure I understand. You want me to check recordings of board and stockholder meetings and anything else I can find to sample the voices of Low-Dunn executives fitting your description. And you want me to compare them with this recording to see if I get a match."

"That's right," Liz confirms. "And Ms. Laughlin, I need you to do it as quickly as you can. Every day these people are conspiring with the Schiller campaign. They're threatening the health of everyone in this country. Hell! They're threatening the health of this planet."

Laughlin's mouth quirks in a bemused smile. "You're passionate about your cause. I'll give you that."

"Not a tenth as passionate as Nathalie Wellstone is. You may be totally unaware of it, but she's working her ass off for you every single day, and she's been doing it for years. If Low-Dunn puts Schiller in office, you might as well forget about your job. Nathalie expanded funding for public universities. Schiller plans to cut it."

Laughlin crosses her arms in front of her face as if fending off a blow. "All right. I get the picture. Text me your contact information. I'll get back to you as soon as I have anything."

Liz pulls out her phone. "I'll be waiting."

Mary drops herself into the chair at her workstation at Schiller Headquarters. After giving her recording to Liz, she didn't want to come back, but they were both afraid it would look fishy. And she'd have to explain it to Chester. She's been closer to her son in the last week or two than in the past few years. They've had dinner three times without an argument. She's proud of the work she's been doing for Nathalie but terrified of what will happen if Chester finds out. She could lose her son for good.

CHAPTER ELEVEN

"Where the hell did Wellstone get all that video?" Schiller demands angrily. "The comments are painting me as a lunatic."

"It's edited for maximum effect," Rory admits, "but everything there is something you said at a rally. And your followers responded to all of it. If you try to walk it back, Wellstone can claim that you're a liar, and you'll confuse your supporters."

"So, what do we do?" Schiller questions.

"Don't try to answer your attackers at all. Go on the offensive. Use the money from the Low-Dunn PAC to attack Wellstone hard. Things were already moving in that direction anyway. Low-Dunn wants to paint her as a wild-eyed tree-hugging fanatic who will destroy the national budget and bring business to its knees."

"She has been in the Senate for years and hasn't done any of that," Schiller retorts.

"It doesn't matter," Rory counters. "Most of the public doesn't know or care what goes on in the Senate. They'll listen to what they hear in TV commercials and what we feed them on social media. So far, Wellstone is depending on her followers to put out the video for her. And they're doing a damned good job. But the Low-Dunn PAC can fund a blitz. We'll bury her message."

"We need a new chant," Schiller decides. "How about 'Ditch the ditz?'"

Rory shakes his head. "Needs work. I'll put our ad guy on it. But it's a good idea. We'll come up with something short we can put on new hats and T-shirts your hardcore followers will shell out for. We can even raise the price. And we'll need to pack your schedule too. You should do at least two rallies a day until we've got Wellstone's new push under control."

"All right," Schiller agrees, "but I'm going to need some destressing on the trail. How about the new girl, the pretty one with the great ass?"

"Bringing your wife would be better optics," Rory suggests.

"We'll bring her, but she won't care what I'm doing in the back of the bus. She can't resist heavy metal, and we have an arrangement. One of the Alpha Wolves is servicing her. She'll wave supportively from the stage. Then the bike boy can screw her brains out. She won't care what I do."

"As long as the press and the Wellstone campaign don't get wind of your 'arrangement,'" Rory cautions. "You're running on family values. Wellstone's got to be the immoral bitch."

Schiller jams his thumbs under his belt. "Don't worry about it."

Nathalie pales as Liz runs Schiller's latest ad on her iPad. "How could he say that? How could anyone even think that? I've never done anything like that in my life."

"The truth doesn't matter to Schiller," Liz reminds her. "He'll keep repeating the lie until people take it as gospel."

Nathalie shudders. "It sounds like something the Ministry of Truth would do in '1984.'"

"Or something Goebbels did in 1944," Liz replies grimly.

"So, how do we get out in front of it?" Nathalie demands.

Her fingers curled in a death grip around her tablet, Liz shakes her head. "I don't know. But I do have experience with shameless liars like Schiller. They accuse their enemies of the crimes they commit themselves. If he's painting you as a brazen whore, there's a good chance he's fooling around himself. Secrets like that have a way of leaking out."

Chester proudly assumes his position near Schiller's bus. Usually, the Alpha Wolves make sure no one disturbs the candidate until he's ready to come out to share with his followers. But one of them didn't show up, and Chester was tagged to take his place.

No one will get near that vehicle if Chester can help it. And he's willing to put his life on the line to make sure. He was going to meet his mother at the sales table, but nothing could be more important than taking care of Schiller.

Chester spots a young woman approaching the entrance to the transport. It's only natural. A lot of the ladies are drawn by Schiller's magnetism. Chester expects that the Alpha Wolf blocking the door will turn her away, but the guard smiles and pulls out a walkie-talkie. When the door opens, he helps her up the steps.

Confused, Chester tries to figure out what happened. Finally, he convinces himself that the girl must be one of Schiller's relatives, a niece, or something. The candidate is devoted to his family. He says so often enough. And his wife is always on stage with him. Chester didn't see her get on the bus. She must have somewhere else essential to be. But what could be more important than being with her husband? She and Schiller have the perfect marriage. Chester will figure it out. He just needs to think about it for a while.

Mary arrived two hours before Schiller's rally to organize the tables selling T-shirts and hats. She's no authority on fashion, but her experience doing thousands of loads of laundry tells her which clothes hold up to multiple washings. This crap won't. The labels inside say, "Made in the U.S.A.," but the paperwork shows they're from the Marianas Islands. She's heard about the sweatshops there. The media filmed exposes of virtual slaves sewing celebrity clothing lines. It figures. Schiller wouldn't mind inflicting misery to make a profit any more than Low-Dunn does.

At least she'll get to spend more time with Chester. He didn't say what it was but bragged about having an important assignment for Schiller. He and Mary are supposed to meet after the rally for a late dinner. If she's really lucky, he may tell her something Nathalie can use. But she's looking forward to sharing a meal with him whether he does or not.

Country music begins to pour from speakers, and the crowd gathers in front of the stage. Rory Montrose comes out to warm them up and lead the chants, during which Schiller usually appears to his disciples' ecstatic cheers. Rory glances back at the curtains behind the stage. It's way past the time when Schiller usually makes his entrance, and the crowd is getting restless.

Schiller's supporters erupt in screams and applause when he finally shows up. Mary pulls out her phone and activates the zoom. Is Schiller's fly open? Rory grabs him in a man-hug and whispers in his ear as they step behind a curtain for a moment. If Schiller was undone, he isn't now, but Mary's pretty sure what she saw. And she has it on her cell.

"I'm sorry," Chester apologizes as he trots over to meet his mother. "An Alpha Wolf was supposed to come to relieve me, but no one showed up. And Mrs. Schiller didn't arrive either. Finally, Mr. Schiller's driver told me he was ready to go, and I could take off. Maybe they're going to pick Mrs. Schiller up somewhere. Mr. Schiller still had a guest on the bus with him, maybe his niece or something."

"They'll probably have a nice little get-together later," Mary assures her son, fingering the phone in her pocket. No wife, open zipper, and an unidentified female guest. She doesn't know what Liz can do with that information and the picture of Schiller's pants. Nathalie always likes to take the high road. Still, if Schiller is cheating on his wife, his followers, especially the religious ones, have a right to know. But Mary wants to spend some time with Chester before she deals with that. "I saw a diner just down the road. Want to try it?" she suggests to her son. "They had a picture of cherry pie on the sign."

Chester smacks his lips. "Sounds great."

CHAPTER TWELVE

"There's no way we can use what Mary brought you, Liz," Nathalie declares. "We would be throwing accusations at Schiller without any proof. That would make us no better than he is."

"I get that," Liz agrees. "So does Mary. But it offers confirmation of what we suspected. Schiller is probably as much of a sleaze in his personal life as he is in his political campaign. If this does become public, some of his followers will find his behavior impossible to accept. And if that does happen, it will make it easier for you to fight the crap he's been dumping on you. Suppose he is exposed in the press or even by one of his faithful. In that case, we'll need to have our ducks in a row for handling the situation without descending to his level."

Nathalie crosses her arms across her chest, the muscles popping at the hinge of her jaw. "Whatever we do, we're not wallowing in the mud with him. We tell the truth. That's all. We keep telling it."

A deep sigh deflates Liz's chest. "It's not going to be easy."

Nathalie sinks into a chair. "Nothing about this campaign is."

Chester is so proud he can hardly stand it. A member of Rory Montrose's staff asked him if he'd like to work for the campaign for pay. It's not much money, but he wasn't earning big bucks on his regular job, either. Chester will get to go to rallies all over the state, two a day, filling in wherever he's needed.

He has to sign a non-disclosure saying he won't reveal anything confidential he sees or hears, but he could never betray Schiller that way. No way is Chester going to let anything that Nathalie Wellstone could use to her advantage slip out.

He'll be starting right away, filling in for one of the Alpha Wolves. He barely has time to pack. But during his stint in prison, he learned he could get along without much stuff. As long as he doesn't have to keep checking who's behind him and he can eat a decent meal now and then, he'll be happy. He might even find another diner that serves cherry pie. Staff at Chester's low level don't get to ride on the bus with Mr. Schiller. Chester's not sure what he'd say to the great man if he got the chance anyway. He'll be in a van on the road, take his turn driving and get his assignment when he arrives. In fact, he'll be meeting the others at the vehicle in two hours.

Mary isn't sure whether to be disappointed or thrilled when Chester brags that he'll be part of Schiller's paid retinue. Mary will be absorbing every word he tells her about it. Still, Chester will be even more vulnerable to Schiller's brainwashing. She mentally crosses her fingers and congratulates him. She'll have to tell Liz, but she also still has to make a living.

It's time for Mary's shift at the toy store. More customers, especially grandparents, are coming in wearing Schiller hats. She sold some of them herself at Schiller rallies, but her stomach still clenches every time she sees one. The last thing Mary wants is to strengthen Schiller's war chest or see his following increase.

Chester grins as he hops aboard the crowded van. Only, as far as he can tell, it's meant to seat 10, but there are at least 14 people inside. Some of the women are sitting on men's laps. They don't seem to mind, but for as long as he can remember, Chester's mom and dad always taught him that everyone in a moving vehicle should wear seatbelts. It's bad enough that some buses don't have any, but there's really no excuse in a van this small.

Chester wonders if Mr. Schiller knows about the unsafe conditions for his staff. Chester decides that he must not, or he would put a stop to them. Their leader is a wonderful man. He wouldn't want anything bad to happen to any of them, would he? Chester's sure it's just an oversight. The campaign will fix it as soon as there's a chance.

One of the guys starts singing a song parody about Nathalie Wellstone. The words are nasty and dirty. Chester doesn't like that either. Nathalie Wellstone may be a terrible woman, but Schiller's followers are supposed to be good people. They shouldn't say things like that.

For a second, Chester wonders if he's made a mistake. Maybe Schiller isn't what his disciple thought he was. No. That's impossible! Some people in the campaign might screw up, but not Schiller. Schiller's perfect. And he's going to save the country from destruction. Of that, Chester is sure.

Mary luxuriates in her shower. With Schiller working the crowds at the other end of the state, she has some time to herself. But at the pace she's been going lately, her feet may be still, but her mind isn't. It's been a long time since she's heard from Doctor Lawrence, or at least it seems like a long time. He told her that for research with as profound implications as a "believe gene," everything has to be checked, rechecked, and checked some more before the idea stands a chance of acceptance by the scientific community. Still, she's impatient.

Lawrence isn't the only one not keeping in touch. With more than a tinge of guilt, Mary realizes that it's been weeks since she talked to Lily Rostoff. That's something she needs to fix. And she will, as soon as she finishes her shower.

After napping in too tight a space, Chester wakes up with cramped muscles. He checks his watch. He's been asleep for almost two hours, and he and Schiller's other staff members should be arriving at the venue soon.

The rally won't be until morning, but they have a lot to do, clearing an area, establishing a secure perimeter, and setting up chairs and tables. So Chester doesn't expect to get more sleep. He doesn't even know if he and his co-workers will be provided with sleeping quarters. When time is tight, Mr. Schiller usually stays on his bus. Chester's heard there are nice beds and even a shower in there, but he's never been aboard to find out. Maybe if he works hard enough, he'll see it sometime.

The van pulls to a stop in an outdoor arena parking area, and a campaign supervisor bangs on the sliding door. "It's time to move your butts."

The arena lights blaze, creating almost a daylight brilliance. As quickly as the stiffness in his legs will allow, Chester springs out of the vehicle, full of enthusiasm for the work ahead. "Taxtrum, after you're finished working setup, you'll be part of the detail guarding the big bus," the site manager announces. Chester has earned that honor for a second time. He can hardly wait.

Standing at the post he'd assumed before, Chester notices the woman he'd previously seen, getting off the bus and heading into the arena. She must have come with Mr. Schiller. The candidate and his wife should be getting off the vehicle any time too. The rally is scheduled to start soon. He watches anxiously to see Schiller emerge. The candidate finally does but without his wife. That's strange. Chester would have thought she'd be on the bus with him for the long trip. The cousin, or whoever she is, was along. A funny feeling stirs in Chester's stomach, but he ignores it. Maybe Mrs. Schiller wasn't feeling well. Chester hopes she's better soon.

CHAPTER THIRTEEN

Remembering to check his fly before he takes the stage, Schiller is feeling good. His new lay doesn't just have a great ass; she's got stamina. He had a great trip to - wherever this is. He'll just have to be careful not to refer to the location. His stump speech is pretty much the same, whatever the venue, as long as he can tell urban or rural. And he has to watch his language around the evangelicals. But Rory always gives him a heads up when the religious nuts are around. The campaign manager has someone survey the parking lot for church buses and fish bumper stickers. He didn't issue any warnings this morning, so things should be pretty free and easy.

As the applause and whistles go on and on, Schiller bathes in the glow. His followers love him. He can feed them any kind of bull, and they'll lap it up like a kitten with cream. From the corner of his eye, he sees the new girl smiling from the side of the stage. Damn! She was supposed to watch on a monitor and stay out of sight. Nothing he can do about it right now, but he'll have a talk with her later. The idiots hanging on his every word probably won't notice.

While standing guard at the big bus, Chester can't see Schiller, but his voice is loud and clear on the P.A. system. There isn't much that Chester hasn't heard before, but the repetition of the message is reassuring and energizing.

He watches the lead guard, who is, of course, an Alpha Wolf, allow another Alpha Wolf to board the bus. Chester doesn't know why the new arrival is there, but it could be some kind of security sweep. Nathalie Wellstone seems to get a lot of information about the campaign, and Schiller likes to make sure he isn't being bugged. It would be disgraceful to plant a microphone in Schiller's private sleeping quarters. But then Wellstone could be capable of anything.

Not long after the Alpha Wolf gets aboard, Mrs. Schiller arrives. She looks a little flushed to Chester. Maybe she's still sick or something and wants to lie down on the bus. She has a few words with the guard at the door, but Chester is too far away to hear what they're saying, especially over Schiller's speech. The guard looks unsure as he lets Mrs. Schiller in. Chester has no idea why the Wolf would be, but then there are many things he's at too low a level to know.

That's all right. Mrs. Schiller is where she belongs. Chester's sure that Mr. Schiller will be glad to see her when he finishes with the rally. The big man always says that God gave him his perfect match. God can't be wrong.

As soon as the cheering for his speech dies down, Schiller disappears behind the curtain. He reaches out to drag the new girl behind it with him. "You're supposed to stay out of sight, or at least lose yourself in the crowd. Wellstone's people will be monitoring all the videos. What if they see you standing there and put two and two together? We could have one hell of a mess."

"I wasn't doing anything," she protests. "I just look like an enthusiastic fan." She reaches toward his belt buckle. "Which I am."

"Not in public, you're not. Look, my wife doesn't care. You know that. But if we're going to make this campaign work, I have to keep up my image as the faithful family man. I can't even be seen in a room with a woman unless my wife is there. I'll take care of you. Just show some discretion. My wife's going to be on stage with me at the next stop. She should have been at this one. You can ride with Rory. We'll get together after and have a good time. Can you deal with that?"

"I guess," Schiller's erstwhile partner answers sullenly. "But one of these times, I want you all to myself."

"Not during this push, but I'll see what we can work out," Schiller promises. He's already considering what it will take to get rid of her. But at this point, it would probably be too much hassle and risk. So he'll have to keep her on the hook - for now.

Chester is over the moon at his assignment to guard the bus again at the next rally. It's hard on his feet, just standing there, but it's worth it. He watched with relief as Mr. Schiller joined his wife for the short trip to the next site.

He'll also be put on set-up duty again. It's going to be a very long day, but it will be worth it. Schiller should be able to pick up a lot of votes. What could be better than that? Still, Chester's hoping that he'll be able to grab some sleep without waking up cramped. Maybe he'll be assigned to a different van. He remembers that he promised his mom he'd tell her how things are going. He's not allowed to use his phone on duty, and he's surrounded aboard the vehicles. But he'll figure something out.

Mary hasn't heard from Chester. Given his pride in serving that bastard Schiller, it worries her that he hasn't called to boast. They're probably keeping him too busy. The problem is that when Chester gets tired, his mouth tends to run away with him. He'll mean well, but he means well working for Schiller too. And he couldn't have chosen a worse idol.

She logs onto YouTube, grimacing as she watches the most recent video of a Schiller rally. She doesn't see anything new, except for a brief look of annoyance on the slimy pol's face when he glances toward the side of the stage. It reminds her of the expression on some of her co-workers when they spot a demanding customer. So Nathalie's opponent could be having a little problem. That might not be much, but it's something. In Mary's experience, when someone trying to make a sale screws up, they keep making a mess of things.

There's nothing she can do about that now except wait to hear from Chester and keep up with the video except - guilt invades her reverie. She still hasn't called Lily. It's late in the day to do that, but she can send her an email.

On an impulse, Mary uses her sign-in to check the Schiller campaign's customer list. Damn! Evan Rostoff is on it for multiple items. He's also thoroughly caught up in the insanity. That's even more reason why Mary and Lily should keep in close touch. The well-being of both their sons hangs in the balance. Screw the time. She'll call Lily anyway.

Chester aches all over when he collapses onto one of the cots the campaign provided for lower-level workers. He's too tired to even know where they are but guesses that it's the overflow area for some venue. In a few hours, he'll be setting up the chairs. But for now, all he wants to do is sleep. And he hopes the campaign will come up with some food, too.

He wakes up to an almost depleted stack of sandwiches and packets of chips on a table, along with a red punch that looks like what he had at camp when he was a kid. He hated it then, but now he can't wait to chug as much of it as he can get. At least the buzz from the sugar will get him going again. He's grateful for that.

CHAPTER FOURTEEN

"I'm happy you called," Lily confesses. "Evan barely talks about anything but Schiller. And he never goes anywhere without that stupid hat. I wish I could burn the thing. I don't know what to say to him. I can't agree with the venom that man spouts, but I don't want to push my son away either. I just cook for him. I think he's gained the ten pounds I've lost worrying about him."

"I know what you mean," Mary sympathizes. "I have all the ingredients for cherry pie on hand in case Chester is around long enough to eat one. But Schiller keeps him busy. He must work at least 14 hours a day with no overtime pay. And at his wages, that's slavery. He says he's happy, but I'm not so sure. I think he's beginning to have some doubts about Schiller. But he's not about to admit them, even to himself. Still, that's a change. He's never doubted anything before. Maybe the exhaustion has something to do with it."

"Doctor Lawrence or Doctor Greenspan might have an idea about that," Lily suggests.

"Yeah," Mary considers. "It can't hurt to ask. And it's earlier in California where Lawrence is."

"We've identified many factors that affect epigenetics, Ms. Taxtrum," Doctor Lawrence explains. "You're well aware of one of them, environmental pollutants. We're also looking at such elements as diet, obesity, physical activity, tobacco smoking, alcohol consumption, psychological stress, and working nights."

"The, um, subject isn't drinking or smoking, but I don't think he's eating decent meals, and he's working practically around the clock. Could that really change the way the believe gene works?" Mary inquires.

"We don't have enough evidence for me to say definitively one way or another," Lawrence replies. "But what you describe could create conditions that would modify his behavior. Can you keep me in the loop about his continuing reactions?"

"I will," Mary promises.

Chester's lost track of where he is or even what day it is. At every stop, he hears almost the same speech from Schiller. He sets up chairs, guards the bus, and eats and sleeps when he can. That's not often. Because he's using a different hole in his belt, he thinks he's losing weight. After a rally, he's often too tired to eat the food provided. And it hasn't been that great anyway.

Schiller's cousin, or whoever she is, hasn't been around much. Chester thought he saw her getting into Rory's car a couple of times, but she hasn't been on the bus. Mrs. Schiller's been on the bus more, and the Alpha Wolf who's been with her has joined her at a few stops. That's what Chester thinks, anyway. He's not sure of the comings and goings anymore. He's not sure of much, except that he'd give almost anything for a whole night's sleep in a regular bed and a slice of cherry pie. At the moment, he can't see having a chance at either.

Rory calls for the attention of the assembled staff. "I want to thank you all for the wonderful job you've been doing. As some of you may know, our leader has been rising in the polls. That means that even more patriotic citizens will want to come out to hear what he has to say. It also means that you'll be working harder than ever. It's time for the big push.

"We'll be moving from two stops every 24 hours to three. That means you'll have a lot more setting up to do, and you'll have to do it faster. But we'll also have a special reward for you. Street Treat food trucks have come aboard with the campaign. We'll have one at every stop, and you'll each be able to get whatever you want. I'm told that the company serves great meatball sandwiches but specializes in pie."

A thrill runs through Chester. He likes meatball sandwiches, but the vision of a slice of cherry pie hovers before his eyes. Schiller couldn't be a greater man. Finally, Chester will have exactly what his hungry body's been craving. So what if he has to work harder for it?

The line in front of the food truck stretches for half the length of a football field, but Chester's willing to take his place in it. By now, he's used to standing - for hours sometimes. At least in line, he gets to move around a bit.

Chester's right behind an Alpha Wolf, the one who boarded the bus with Mrs. Schiller. He pays no attention to Chester, leaving the minor staff member's nod unrecognized. Chester finds being ignored a little annoying, but the Alpha Wolves are Schiller's choice to rule the roost. So nothing Chester thinks about them should matter. Schiller knows best, right?

The scent of the cherry pie the wolf orders to top off his triple burger and fries tantalizes Chester's senses. He can almost taste it. "Sorry, just gave away the last slice," the truck's server informs him when he orders one of his own.

Anger flashes through Chester like flame through the tinder in the campfires he made as a kid. All he wanted was the damn pie, and he can't have it. It isn't fair! He works as hard as an Alpha Wolf. Harder! And all he gets is sore feet and an empty stomach. Damn Schiller! Damn the campaign anyway. He wants to go home!

By the time Chester takes his place on guard duty, he's calmed down a bit, but he doesn't have as easy a time accepting what he sees. The Alpha Wolf is on the bus with Mrs. Schiller again, and Chester heard the woman riding with Rory complaining that she wanted some time alone with her man. Chester doesn't want to think about what she means by that.

He takes a moment to consider his finances. They aren't getting any better working on the Schiller campaign. He's always hungry and tired, and he didn't even get his damn pie.

He quit his old job, but he can get one cleaning up in the restaurant below where he still has his tiny apartment. He won't be doing great, but he won't be starving. The restaurant isn't bad, and it lets employees eat in the kitchen. He'll save some money that way. And he can grab a few meals with his mother. He needs to talk about what he's been seeing, and he wouldn't feel right talking to anyone else. That's it. After the campaign gives him what there is of his pay, he'll leave.

Mary throws her arms around her son. "I'm so glad you came home."

"He didn't let us sleep, and I didn't get enough to eat," Chester complains. "It was worse than prison. I know you like him, Mom, but I saw some things that shouldn't have happened. I don't think he's the man we thought he was."

"I saw a few things that bothered me too," Mary confides, carefully leaving out passing anything on to the Wellstone campaign. "You want to tell me what you saw?"

"Sure," Chester agrees. "But can we order a pizza first? I'm starving."

"You're home now. You can have whatever you want," Mary assures her son. "And you can tell me all about what upset you, just like you did when you were a little boy."

Chester sinks into a nearby chair. "I'd like that. I'd like it a lot."

Mary pulls her cellphone out of the pocket of her slacks. "Good, what do you want on your pizza?"

Chester grins. "Pepperoni, sausage, mushrooms, peppers, and extra cheese."

Mary can't help smiling at her son's eagerness. "Sounds great."

CHAPTER FIFTEEN

Her friends might call her Merry, but Meredith Brookhauser hasn't been so pissed off in her life. Schiller assured her that she was the best lover he'd ever had. Behind the scenes, he was going to leave his wife to be with her. She just had to be patient. But the more patient she was, the worse things got.

And the last time Merry tried to see her man, that sonofabitch Alpha Wolf wouldn't let her on the bus. He said Mrs. Schiller was aboard, but Merry knew that wasn't true. She'd seen the motorcycle whore sneak away with another wolf.

Merry stomps off to face down Rory Montrose. "If he doesn't start giving me what I need, I'm going to blow his little charade wide open, I swear!"

"It won't be much longer," Rory soothes. "He just needs to get in another week or two of stops, and then he'll be all yours. He has a cabin by the lake. It will be just the two of you, no campaign, and no speeches."

"You'd better be right," Merry warns. "Two weeks, Rory, and I get what I need, or all his crazy followers who think Ray's the second coming are going to find out just what kind of comings he likes."

"Two weeks," Rory promises.

Rory grabs Schiller's arm as he's descending the stairs from the stage. "I need to talk to you."

"Not now," Schiller protests. "I'm going to press the flesh. I have to keep my supporters engaged."

"If you don't pay attention," Rory cautions, "you're not going to have any supporters. Your little side dish came to me. She thinks she should be the main course, and she's planning to go to the media if she doesn't get more attention."

"I can't do that," Schiller protests. "The idiots at rallies take too many videos. Sooner or later, she's going to show up in them again, and Facebook and Twitter will have a field day. Can't we just put her up out of sight in a security suite of a hotel? I'll tell her that I'll get to her when the campaign calms down."

"We both know the campaign isn't going to calm down," Rory points out. "We've had some of our set-up guys leaving because they claim they're overworked. I've been keeping Meredith on the hook about a trip to your cabin for almost two weeks. I can't keep promising anymore. She could shoot off her mouth anytime. Look, Ray, if you can't handle this, we'll need to call in some help. I can put Grover on it."

"Do it!" Schiller orders.

"Why the hell couldn't Schiller keep his fly zipped?" Monteith Metzger explodes. "We gave him everything for his damn campaign. He even had his wife along. What did he need with some little piece of ass?"

"Apparently, he didn't need her enough," Grover Norliss explains. "She got possessive and started spouting off at Montrose. She's threatening to go to the tabloids."

"Most of them are on Schiller's side," Metzger considers. "We paid enough to put them there and make up all that crap about Wellstone. But you never know who'll go for a sex scandal. And we have no control over social media. The bitch could put it all out there at any moment with her phone. So what do we do to take care of this before it blows up in our faces? Pay her off?"

"She still might decide to talk," Norliss points out. "A big-mouthed bitch did that to a senator in the last election cycle."

"Then make sure whatever else needs to be done is done," Metzger orders, "but it can't trace back to Low-Dunn or Schiller."

Norliss nods. "I understand."

Ray has a surprise for you," Rory announces to Merry.

Her brows converge in suspicion. "What kind of surprise?"

He wants you at his place on a lake not far from here. It's beautiful, and there won't be any crowds or Alpha Wolves. It'll be just you and Ray for the whole holiday weekend."

Merry's eyes narrow. "Why isn't Ray having rallies over the holiday?"

"Because he supports families and thinks they should spend the time together," Rory explains.

"You must have practiced being able to say that with a straight face, Rory," Merry smirks. "But a lake cabin sounds nice. When are we going?"

"I'll take you there this afternoon. Ray will join you tonight."

"He'd better," Merry warns. "Does the place have food? It's not like we can call room service."

"You'll have everything you need and more," Rory assures her.

"Ray will be here soon," Rory announces as he drops Merry off on the paved area in front of a cabin. He drives away as she's going inside.

She gazes around the love nest Ray chose for their extended weekend. She has to admit that it isn't bad. The small kitchen has up-to-date appliances. Area rugs cover wood plank floors, and the bathroom has both a shower and a large tub. Sets of Egyptian cotton towels hang on a rack, and the bedsheets are a high thread count. An armoire provides more than enough room for the clothes in her suitcase, and the refrigerator is fully stocked, including two bottles of Dom Perignon. "Not bad, Ray," she murmurs to the empty air. "Who'd you con into giving you this place?"

Delighted to find that the cabin has a workable Wi-Fi signal, Merry scrolls through postings on a fashion website. When the temperature in the cottage rises, she decides to indulge herself with the high-priced champagne. She and Ray will still have one bottle left to share.

After two glasses of bubbly, Merry's eyelids begin to droop, and she stretches out on the bed. She'll rest for just a little while to be fresh when Ray arrives.

Two men in an unmarked black SUV pull in and park where Rory's car had been. One of them peeks through the window of the cabin. "She must have gotten into the doped wine. She's out. Let's go get her." He pulls out a key to the door.

The two intruders carry Merry 200 feet to a boat tied at a pier on the lake Rory had extolled. "The middle is the deepest part. That's where we should dump her," the second man suggests, wrapping a weight belt around Merry's waist. "If anyone ever finds her, it will be too late to get any evidence off the body. And with the number of cabins with piers, it will be impossible to connect her with Schiller or the company."

His partner nods his agreement, steering to the suggested area. The two men readily toss Merry over the side, and she sinks out of sight. The boat's motor guns and they retreat from their task.

The cold liquid shocks Merry alert. She's at home in the water. As practice for holding a pose, she was on a synchronized swimming team. Fighting to surface, she realizes that the belt around her waist is holding her down. She grapples with the catch until it finally releases and propels herself upward with powerful kicks. A boat with two men in it is moving toward the shore. The image burns into her mind.

As she recovers, floating on the surface of the water, full realization penetrates Merry's waterlogged brain. Someone meant for her to never make it out of this lake alive. Could the men in the boat be who tried to kill her? If they were, she can guess who sent them. Schiller, Montrose, those sons of bitches! They lied. Schiller wanted to get rid of her - forever. Well, he didn't! She's going to live and make it to shore. And she's going to make Ray Schiller regret every breath he takes.

CHAPTER SIXTEEN

Merry has no idea in which direction the cabin lies. She isn't sure she wants to go there anyway. It could be where her would-be killers decide to dock the boat. She scans the shore in the distance and strikes out for the spot that looks the closest.

The chill of the water is enervating, and her legs begin to feel as if they're loaded with the lead in her discarded belt. The sun is shining brightly, and she lies on her back for a few moments absorbing its rays before beginning to swim again. By the time she reaches the shore, except for uncontrollable shivering, she can barely move. But she's not about to give up. Forcing herself to her feet, she pictures every step she takes as a kick to Ray's most sensitive spot. Finally, she spies a cabin with lights on. Falling to her knees in front of the door, she beats her fists against the wood.

It seems an eternity until Merry hears someone coming. She finds herself staring up at a small girl. All she can make out are long braids and a very open mouth.

"Mom!"

Merry hears the smack of flip-flops against wood.

"Omigod!

"I need help," Merry rasps.

The woman backs away from the door, pulling her daughter with her. "Who are you? What happened to you?"

Merry struggles to her feet. "My name is Meredith Brookhauser. Two men tried to drown me in the lake. Please, can you call the police?"

"Out here, it's the sheriff," the woman informs her. "But damn straight, I'll call him. I'll lend you a blanket, but you stay out there until he comes."

"All right," Merry agrees. "Just tell him to hurry."

"You can bet on that."

"So Merry's dead?" Schiller demands.

"That's what Norliss told me," Rory reports. "I took her to the cabin at the lake, but I don't want to know any more than that."

Schiller's fingers curl into tight fists. "I hope Grover's people cleaned up after themselves."

"He's always come through for us before," Rory points out.

Schiller shakes his head. "To lean on someone, sure, but never to take anyone out permanently."

"It will be fine," Rory assures his boss. "But you should go update your speech. You've been losing some of your audience in the middle section. And after this, Low-Dunn won't put up with any sliding support."

"I won't make any," Schiller declares. "Next rally, I'll have everyone in the palm of my hand."

"Just make sure they don't slip through your fingers."

Sheriff Jolley stares down at a still-soaked Meredith Brookhauser. "Are you trying to tell me that Ray Schiller's campaign manager delivered you to a cabin where you drank drugged Champagne, and then two men tried to drown you?"

Beneath her soggy blanket, Meredith squares her shoulders. "That's exactly what I'm telling you, Sheriff. How else would I have ended up like this?"

"By getting drunk and trying to swim across the lake," Jolley replies. "I have kids do it every summer."

"At least take me to the hospital so they can test me for drugs," Meredith insists. "And they can test for my alcohol level too. That will prove I didn't get drunk."

"I'll take you to the hospital," Jolley agrees. "The headshrinker might like to have a word with you. Ray Schiller! Like hell! The whole county is planning to vote for him."

"Well, they wouldn't if they knew what I know," Meredith asserts. "The doctors will see I'm telling the truth. And if you don't believe me, I'll find someone who will."

Jolley snorts. "Yeah, sure. Come on then, we'll go see the docs."

"I want that blanket back, Sheriff," the cabin owner yells after them.

"Nice people out here," Merry mutters. "No wonder they love Ray. They're his kind of assholes."

"Mom, look at this!" Chester calls over his second slice of cherry pie.

Mary emerges from the kitchen. "What is it?"

"The news. A woman is claiming that Rory Montrose and Ray Schiller tried to have her killed."

"I'd believe it of Schiller, but people say all kinds of things," Mary offers.

"But I recognize her," Chester protests. "The Alpha Wolves let her on the bus with Schiller - for a while, anyway. And you should recognize her too. She was in the video on Twitter and Instagram. She was the woman standing to the edge of the stage while Schiller was talking to the crowd."

Mary gazes at the TV screen. "I think you're right. But if she was one of Schiller's followers, why would she say a thing like that?"

"Maybe he didn't want her following him anymore." Chester considers. "The Wolves stopped letting her on the bus. Listen, she's giving her Twitter handle. We should tweet her. She might remember me. I was by the bus sometimes when she tried to get on. If she's telling the truth, someone should help her tell everyone what a liar Schiller is. She should at least know that someone believes her."

Mary nods. "Yes, she should."

Merry looks suspiciously at a tweet from Mary Taxtrum, explaining that she and her son want to help get the word out about Schiller. The name Taxtrum rings a bell. She saw it on the nametag of one of Schiller's dupes, who faithfully guarded the bus while the Alpha Wolves strutted around. She also saw him on Rory's roster a couple of times. But she hadn't seen him for a couple of weeks before Schiller tried to take her out. Maybe he got wise and went running home to momma.

Mary proposed a meeting on neutral ground at a toy store. Unless the place sells a different kind of toy, it's nowhere Ray or his minions would go. Merry just might take Mary up on her offer. She needs to get something for her nephew's birthday anyway, and she doesn't have a clue what kids like. Maybe the lady can help. She not only seems to like toy stores, but she also has a son. Meeting up with her just might work out.

Mary checks the response from Meredith Brookhauser. She hadn't expected the woman to agree to meet, but she's grateful that she did, both for her sake and Nathalie Wellstone's. Schiller might finally have gone too far.

Mary leads the way to a back room with shelves full of out-of-season toys. "No one will bother us here, but I only have 20 minutes for my break, so I'll have to make this short. I remember seeing you at a Schiller rally. I got you on video looking at him like he was the most important man on earth."

"I felt that way about him- for a while," Merry confesses. "But the more I got to know him, the more I realized that he doesn't care about anyone but himself. He wants money and power, and he doesn't care what he says or who he hurts to get it. So I'm going to the press. But I need as many people to back me up as I can get."

"Can you prove Schiller tried to kill you?" Mary inquires.

"Not yet. Not enough for criminal charges. But I can bring a civil suit. That means I'll get discovery, and I can start digging. I was hoping that you and your son could help me figure out where to look."

"I don't know what we can tell you that you don't already know," Mary confides. "But I saw some things, and Chester saw more. We'll do what we can."

"Senator Wellstone, a reporter shouts. "What do you think about the suit Meredith Brookhauser is bringing against Ray Schiller?"

Nathalie keeps her voice neutral. "I'm not in possession of the facts, so I'm not in a position to make an evaluation. And when the evidence is revealed in court, the jury will have to decide whether Ms. Brookhauser is eligible for damages. What I can tell you is that the accusations Schiller has thrown at me are completely made up. He is far from demonstrating his honesty."

"So you believe Meredith Brookhauser?" the reporter presses.

"I didn't say that," Nathalie responds. "But I don't disbelieve her. The facts will emerge."

"And when they do?" the reporter continues.

"It will be up to the voters to make a choice," Nathalie declares.

"Very well done," Liz comments off-camera. "You made Schiller sound guilty without saying he was."

"Except of lying about me," Nathalie points out. "He put a target on my back, and now the situation is reversed."

"And you're loving every minute of it."

"Yes," I have to admit I am."

CHAPTER SEVENTEEN

Chester hesitates before picking up another slice of pizza. "Mom, I've decided something."

"What?" Mary asks.

"I need to fix what I messed up. I believed so much in Ray Schiller that I put everything I had into supporting him. I made excuses for him. I went without food. I was always tired. And I did it all for the wrong person. If everything Ray Schiller said was a lie, then everything Nathalie Wellstone said was the truth."

"I think so," Mary agrees. "But you're already helping fix things, Chester. Meredith Brookhauser has the information you gave her. She can use it in court."

"I know," Chester acknowledges, "but I looked it up. Court can take forever, years sometimes. By then, the election will be over, and Ray Schiller could be a senator. He could destroy all the good things Nathalie did. He could make things worse instead of better. I can't let that happen."

"So, what do you want to do?" Mary asks.

"You're already volunteering for Nathalie Wellstone. I want to work for her too. I know how to do things on a campaign. I can set up chairs, sell stuff, anything. I'll work really hard. You know I will."

Mary nods. "Yes, I do."

"Can you get me in?" Chester wonders.

"I think Nathalie will take anyone willing to help, but," Mary promises, "I'll talk to her campaign manager just to check."

Chester picks up his pizza. "Great!"

The brow furrows Liz tries to minimize deepen. "Mary, is this the same son in the study you had Nathalie check out?"

Mary's stomach clenches. "I only have one son. And I admit Chester worked for Schiller. But he found out first hand just what Schiller is, and he wants to make up for it. So he'll be absolutely committed to helping Nathalie win."

Liz lays a hand on Mary's shoulder. "I'm sure he will, but for how long? He turned on Schiller. How do I know he won't turn on Nathalie?"

"When he left Schiller, it was because of what Doctor Lawrence called physical and psychological stressors that affected his condition. Schiller's campaign treated him like dirt. And even then, it wasn't until he saw Meredith Brookhauser and realized that at least some of what she claimed was true that he decided he needed to come work for Nathalie. He knows he did something wrong, and he desperately wants to make it right. So please give him a chance."

Liz's teeth dig into her bottom lip. "I'm going to have to take it to Nathalie. I'll let you know what she decides."

"When?" Mary asks. "He really wants to get to work."

"I'll talk to her tonight," Liz promises.

Nathalie hesitates several times before picking up the phone but finally decides to take the plunge. "Doctor Greenspan, this is Nathalie Wellstone. Do you remember me?"

Greenspan straightens in her chair behind her desk. "Of course I remember you, Senator. And I'm grateful for your support of research funding."

"It's step one in keeping our country at the cutting edge of discovery," Nathalie declares. "But I'm not calling about funding. I'm calling about one of your subjects in your research with Doctor Lawrence."

"Senator, you of all people should understand how vital confidentiality is in maintaining the privacy of the subjects of studies. You've spent more time investigating research conditions than anyone in Congress."

"I do understand," Nathalie assures the researcher. "And I respect it. But I also have to make a decision. So, can we go with a hypothetical?"

"We can try," Greenspan allows.

"Fine," Nathalie agrees. "Suppose one of the subjects was obsessed with supporting my opponent. However, through various forms of physical and psychological abuse at my opponent's hands, he became vulnerable to changing his mind. As a result, he wants to work for me as obsessively as he did for the opposition. Would that be a safe situation for me and, more importantly, for him?"

Greenspan whistles breathily through pursed lips. "So the hypothetical subject wants a chance to redeem himself for past behavior?"

"Essentially."

"In my experience, the need for redemption is a strong motivating force for anyone," Greenspan shares. "Theoretically, I would say you'd be giving him a gift by letting him try. But I would caution you about being careful what you and anyone who interacts with him discloses, um, hypothetically. However, it could be a highly positive experience for both of you."

Nathalie smiles into the phone. "Hypothetically understood, Doctor."

Chester can't believe that while working for Nathalie, he got a slice of pizza while it was still hot. And it wasn't stale either. He worked hard to set up the stage, but he got to rest afterward, and the campaign always has bottled water handy - the kind without the crap that can leach out of the plastic. Every minute, it becomes clearer to him how little Schiller cares about his supporters. Nathalie is more like a classroom mom, taking care of everyone.

An old-timey folk singer's been performing for the crowd. Chester never heard of her before, but his mom did. She said that musicians like that were part of the civil rights movement. Nathalie was too, but she was younger than Chester when she first marched. He's just about to get to hear his first whole speech from Nathalie and couldn't be more excited.

Before Schiller spoke, Rory used to go out to get the crowd to chant nasty things about Nathalie being a crook and belonging in jail. Liz doesn't do that about Schiller. She just talks about the wonderful things Nathalie's done for people and how she'd like to do more of them. She doesn't even mention Schiller. That's fine with Chester. He's had enough of Schiller to last a lifetime.

Gazing into the crowd, Chester suddenly spots a familiar face. For a moment, he can't place it. Finally, he realizes that he's never seen the man before without Alpha Wolf leathers. What is an Alpha Wolf doing here?

Carefully scanning more faces, Chester spots several other wolves, including the pack leader. Acid churns in the pit of his stomach. He has to tell someone - fast. He looks around for his crew chief but can't spot her.

Liz, Nathalie's campaign manager, is surrounded by a press of supporters. Chester can't get to her, either. He has no choice. He'll have to confront a wolf himself. And if the gang is planning something, the pack leader is the only one that can stop them.

Chester's heart is beating a mile a minute. He remembers the name of the Alpha Wolf pack leader. He could hardly have missed it, emblazoned both across the back of the leader's jacket and on the saddlebag of his motorcycle. Chester takes a deep breath before approaching him. "Mitch Degussa, I need to talk to you."

Mitch takes in the Nathalie Wellstone T-shirt hanging on Chester's thin frame and the terrified expression above it. If they were out on the street, he'd just knock the jerk out of the way, but he doesn't want to attract too much attention before the pack is ready to move. "You've got the wrong guy."

Chester shakes his head, the clip holding his badge to the lanyard around his neck rattling with the motion. "No, I don't. I worked on Schiller's campaign long enough to know what he is. And if you're here to make trouble, just forget it, because I know exactly who you are."
Dark confidence glitters in Mitch's eyes. "And what makes you think you'll live long enough to tell anyone?"

"Because I've watched you," Chester replies. "You're lazy. You let the others do the work for you. And you never do anything unless you have your pack to back you up. That makes you a coward. And you work for someone just like you. So whatever you do, I'll let the good people here know exactly who you are and who you work for."

Mitch snarls, charging at Chester. "Like hell, you will!"

Chester strikes the ground with Mitch on top of him, almost hitting several members of the crowd. As a murmur rises, Nathalie looks down from the stage. "What's going on?"

"That asshole jumped on that guy," A woman yells from the crowd.

Gathering his legs to his chest, Chester kicks Mitch away. "He's an Alpha Wolf!" Chester pants, trying to catch his breath. "He works for Ray Schiller. Other Wolves are here too."

Nathalie signals to Liz. "We need to sort this out. I want to talk to both of them."

Sitting in a folding chair in front of Nathalie, Chester focuses his eyes on the ground. "You're Mary Taxtrum's son, aren't you?" Nathalie asks.

Chester keeps his head down. "Yes."

"And you worked for Ray Schiller, didn't you?"

Heat rises in Chester's face. "I did. I'm sorry. I believed him."

Nathalie nods her understanding. "I know you did. A lot of people believed him. A lot of people still do."

"But he's lying!" Chester blurts out. "He wants to hurt people. He wants to hurt you. That's why he sent the Alpha Wolves."

"Look at me, Chester," Nathalie demands. He slowly raises his head. "I believe you. And my security people are turning the Alpha Wolf who attacked you over to the police. What he did is on video from about 20 cell phones. But you're still going to need to talk to a lot of people and answer a lot of questions. Can you do that? Can you do that for me?"

"I can do it for you," Chester promises.

CHAPTER EIGHTEEN

When he was little, Chester fantasized about being a hero on TV. He wanted to go after the bad guys and bring them to justice. He was too young to worry about getting the girl, but for sure, he wanted the admiration. Of course, he always wanted to prove he was right, too. But now that a camera looms, he wishes he was anywhere else.

The reporter interviewing him works for a local morning show. There may not even be that many people watching. Still, he's nervous. How can he explain how he could fall for the garbage Schiller was selling? Nathalie told him to just tell the truth. Then he'll never have to be sorry about anything he says. She does interviews all the time. She must know what she's talking about. At least Chester hopes so.

The seat Chester takes across from morning anchor Dina Vane is much closer to her than it looks on TV. Their knees are almost touching as she leans in to ask her questions. "Chester, I think by now most of our viewers have seen the video of what happened when you spotted Alpha Wolf Mitch Degussa. And that the Alpha Wolves work for Ray Schiller is pretty well known. But the Alpha Wolves are infamous for terrorizing other motorcycle riders and anyone else who decides to get in their way. So can you tell me how you recognized Degussa and why you decided to face him down?"

Chester swallows, feeling sweat break out on his forehead. "I recognized Mitch because before I realized what kind of man Ray Schiller is, I worked for his campaign."

"And what kind of man do you think Schiller is, Chester?" Dina asks.

"I don't think it; I know it," Chester insists. "What Meredith Brookhauser said about being with him is true. I saw her get on his bus. I was helping the Alpha Wolves stand guard. He acts nice, but I know how he treats people. I know how he treated me. He's a liar."

"Chester, you have a troubled history. You were arrested for bringing a gun into a pizzeria and served time. So why should Schiller's supporters trust what you say?"

"Because believing him is what got me in trouble. People on the radio said that perverts in the basement of that pizzeria were hurting kids, and Schiller agreed with them. So I went to save the children, but what Schiller said then was a lie too. There were no children. There wasn't even a basement.

"Schiller tells everyone that Nathalie Wellstone is a terrible person who hurts people and belongs in jail. But that's a lie too. He's the one who hurts people. I've seen it. But Nathalie isn't like that. She wants to help people. That must be why Schiller sent the Wolves."

Dina turns to the camera. "Well, you've heard what Chester had to say. We're on Twitter, Facebook, and Instagram. Let us know what you think. After the break, new foods for your dog."

Mary studies the new Facebook group dedicated to Chester. Some Schindler supporters made nasty posts, but her son has a surprising number of supporters. Some of the young women are even offering dates. Liz warned against taking any of that at face value because the postings could be from bots. Still, the reaction is better than Mary - or Chester - expected. After Dina mentioned his jail time, he was afraid no one would believe him anymore. Instead, it seems to have earned him sympathy, at least from some quarters.

The most encouraging thing to Mary is the call she received from Lily Rostoff. Her friend believes her son Evan may be re-thinking his obsessive support of Schiller. He's not close to supporting Nathalie, but at least what Chester says might have had an impact. Maybe the believe gene effect can be lessened without depriving someone of sleep and starving them half to death. Mary hopes so.

Since his interview with Dina, Chester's gained some confidence. He was on the radio twice, and someone at the restaurant where he works asked him for an autograph. But Liz says not to expect Schiller to give in. Any moment he could put out a new barrage of lies. Mary's sure Nathalie can handle them, but she's less sure about Chester.

Hearing from Lily reminds Mary that she's let things slide with the support group. That Chester is doing better, and Evan may be as well, is encouraging news that she can share. God knows her group hasn't had much of it.

When she calls the church secretary to book the basement, she can almost feel the ice through the phone. "I'm sorry, Mrs. Taxtrum, all the slots in the basement are filled for the next month."

"Well, I suppose it's good to hear that so many people are getting use out of the church," Mary replies.

"Yes, we have a lot of the faithful pursuing meaningful missions."

Mary catches the emphasis on the word "faithful." She knows that much of the congregation holds political views opposed to hers, but it's never been a problem before. At least she didn't think it was a problem. She gazes around her home. Her group doesn't need to meet in a church. She has plenty of space. All she has to do is rearrange some of the furniture in the living room. Chester can help her with that. And she has folding chairs stored in her own basement. If the weather is nice, the group can even meet outside.

She'll be fine. So will Chester. They'll just have to contend with harder heads than she'd figured. With her son, she's been doing that for a long time. She can handle it.

In disgust, Merry turns away from the screen displaying known kidnappers. She glances at Linc Swerdlow, the investigator her lawyer assigned to her case. He's slogging through files at the next desk but knows what she's been doing. "If the cops ever caught those guys, they wouldn't have still been out there. You have the sketches we made. Can't you put them on TV or something?" Merry demands.

"That's likely to drive them underground," Linc explains.

"Then I know a better place to look," Merry asserts. "I'm willing to bet those men worked for Low-Dunn. Isn't there an employee roster or something with pictures?"

"Employee roster, yes. With pictures, not many," Linc replies. "The only photos are of the top executives, the sales staff, and the P.R. guys. I already checked. None of them match your sketches."

"There must be a time employees get together when they take pictures," Merry insists. "Low-Dunn pretends it's a family-friendly company. Their CEO made a big deal of it when he was interviewed on Good Morning U.S.A., calling me a liar. He talked about how wonderful his employees are and how they could never do anything terrible like that to me or anyone else. He also said they'd been at a holiday picnic Low-Dunn arranged for the whole company at the time I was allegedly thrown in the lake. He showed pictures of that. Allegedly," she repeats, "the bastard. He has to know what really happened. But, of course, the guys who dumped me in the water wouldn't have been in those photos."

A smile slowly spreads across Linc's pale face. "Not for this year. But if that picnic is a regular Low-Dunn P.R. event, they could be in some from last year." Moving to Merry's side, he leans in to rapidly tap the keys of her computer. "There! The pictures were posted all over social media. They're still online. Go through them. See if you can find your guys."

"They're not my guys. You can keep them. But I'll look," Merry agrees.

Merry peruses the photographs, nausea beginning to rise in her throat. If she finds the men who tried to drown her, will she be able to face them? She pictures the smug look that will appear on Schiller's face if she backs down. She'll be damned if she'll give him the satisfaction. So she'll do whatever it takes to nail him and Low-Dunn.

Merry is close to the end of the photos when an image of a softball game almost hits her in the face. Crouched behind home plate, in the vulnerable position she wishes she could find him, is one of the men she saw in the boat as it moved away from her. She checks the caption. Rutherford (Rutty) Minger. If he were in front of her right now, he'd have nothing left to rut with. She calls Linc over. "That's one of them." He grins. "That's the start we need to get them both - and the man behind them."

CHAPTER NINETEEN

Only half the chairs in the circle in Mary's living room are filled. Still, she's glad to see the familiar faces. "I suppose you've all heard about what Chester's been doing."

"He's getting his fifteen minutes of fame," one of the women comments. "But is going from total devotion to Ray Schiller to worshipping Nathalie Wellstone really progress? It seems like he traded one obsession for another. I'm not sure that's promising."

"It wasn't a trade," Mary protests. "What I mean is that he was over Schiller before he started believing in Nathalie. Doctor Lawrence thinks that physical stressors were involved. That would mean that interventions might be effective with some of our children."

"Like what deprogrammers used to do with kids pulled in by cults?" Lily Rostoff asks.

"Maybe something like that," Mary considers. "Doctor Lawrence and Doctor Greenspan are still trying to figure out how the process works. But that anything can work at all gives me hope. I pray that all of you can have some as well."

"I'm beginning to," Lily admits. "Evan hasn't had nearly as much of a change of focus as Chester, but he is beginning to doubt. It's been years since once he made up his mind, he could question anything."

"When do you expect to hear more from your experts, Mary?" another parent inquires.

"I don't know," Mary admits. "Doctor Lawrence said he'd stay in touch, but I don't think he knows the timeline himself. So we'll just have to keep our fingers crossed."

"I'd rather curl mine around one of those incredible cookies Mary made," Lily declares. "Anyone want to join me?"

Several of the attendees get up and move toward a nearby table.

Mary draws a deep breath and goes over to pour lemonade.

Rutty Minger looks around as he gets his mail from the receptacle at the curb but doesn't notice Linc. The investigator occupies a car much like the other vehicles on the street and is parked far enough away to be out of Rutty's direct line of vision. Linc arrived just before sunrise, two hours before. But Rutty is still wearing a bathrobe, so he probably hasn't been up long.

As an hourly worker at Low-Dunn, Rutty would be due in at seven a.m. for the morning shift, but he appears to rank higher than that. That's probably how he can afford a house in this neighborhood and the newer model car parked in the driveway. So if Rutty is going into work today, it may not be for a while.

Linc can wait. Not wanting to chance needing a bathroom, he didn't bring coffee. He's never cared for peeing in a bottle or one of the more complex contrivances for the purpose. And he's definitely not crazy about adult diapers. He used the restroom at a gas station a few minutes before he arrived, and it will be at least a couple more hours before he has to relieve himself again.

If he does need to leave, he can set up a camera on the tree that shades Rutty's home. He has one no larger than a shirt button that can transmit over short distances. If Rutty takes off, the camera will note the direction. Linc knows the route to Low-Dunn, and at this point, he won't care much if Rutty goes anywhere else. He wants to find out who Rutty hangs around with at the company. With luck, that will be Merry's other assailant. Even if it isn't, once Linc learns Rutty's routine, he'll be able to follow him anywhere.

Leaning back in his seat, Linc starts his playlist feeding through his car's speakers. It's all high-energy music that would keep dancers on the floor of a club gyrating through the night. He can't afford to doze off, and the driving beat won't let him.

Rutty takes his time getting out of the house but eventually climbs behind the wheel of his car. As his quarry backs out of the driveway, Linc can tell that he's heading in the direction of Low-Dunn. The investigator follows at a distance. Instead of going inside the Low-Dunn complex, Rutty waits in the lot until another man comes to his car.

Parked rows away and displaying a dummied-up Low-Dunn sticker on his back window, Linc watches Rutty through binoculars. He can only see the second man from the side, but Rutty's visitor could match Merry's second sketch. He'll have to wait and see.

Linc picks up his camera and sets the zoom. If he can catch Rutty's buddy close to full-face, even for the fraction of a second it will take him to snap a photo, it will be enough. Then, he can compare it to the sketch at his leisure. And if it's even close, he can show it to Merry.

Merry studies the set of photos Linc laid out in front of her. She picks up a three-quarter view and stares at it. "That's him. That's the way he looked in the boat when the sun hit him. Do you know who he is?"

"I don't have a name," Linc admits. "But this guy and Rutty went into Low-Dunn together. So it shouldn't take too much more work to track down who he is. If we can set them against each other, it will double your chances of proving your case. But don't say anything until we're ready to spring the trap. I think you should go quiet for a while. We don't want to spook them."

"All right," Merry agrees. "I've wanted to take a few days away to get my head together."

Linc nods. "That would be a good idea. If Low-Dunn decides you've backed off, it will be better for you and your case."

Chester forks up tiny nibbles along the edges of his cherry pie. "What's wrong?" Mary asks. "Aren't you feeling well?"

"I feel OK, but I'm worried," he confides. "I haven't seen anything from Meredith Brookhauser on TV or online for days. If she gives up, Schiller will lie even more. He'll say that she was lying all along and that he's innocent. And his followers, most of the people who still show up for his rallies, will believe him."

Mary sighs. "If they're still showing up for his rallies, they'll believe him no matter what she says. We'll just have to work harder to get every vote we can for Nathalie. Liz said that bill Nathalie's pushing through the Senate to get lead out of the drinking water should get a lot of possible voters on her side. We, everybody who works for Nathalie, have to make sure they get to the polls. That will mean knocking on doors, giving rides, or whatever it takes. We're both going to be busy every minute we're not at work."

"I can handle it," Chester declares, digging more enthusiastically into his pie.

His mother nods, smiling. "I know you can."

Schiller slams the lid of his laptop. "I don't want to look at those."

Rory shrugs. "Fine. You can refuse to read the polls, but the numbers are the numbers, whether you accept them or not. We're losing ground. Meredith Brookhauser isn't going to stay quiet long. And we can't go after her again. It would just support what she's been saying.

"And Nathalie Wellstone is beginning to resonate with some of the 'lean Schillers,'" Rory continues. "Her claims about the future she wants for their children and grandchildren are hitting home. And it doesn't help that you've been linked with Low-Dunn. They're not looking that good right now. And they've cut the money stream to a trickle. We're barely funding your rallies, and it's getting worse."

"So, what am I supposed to do?" Schiller demands.

"Cut back on rallies. Instead, use social media to laser-focus our efforts where they will do the most good. We've still got the analytics Low-Dunn funded. We can use them to aim our message at the voters most likely to believe your accusations against Nathalie. We buy what paid ads we can afford and make sure they land in front of the right eyeballs."

"Damn! I love the rallies. I need to get the feedback from my supporters," Schiller protests.

Rory grabs Schiller by the shoulders, forcing him to pay attention. "Ray, you may need the strokes of your adoring crowds, but you need votes a hell of a lot more."

CHAPTER TWENTY

Frown lines deepen in Liz's forehead as she stares at her computer screen. "I don't like the look of these polls. Our general support is growing. But Schiller also got good news. His popularity in some parts of the state has been static or declining ever since Meredith Brookhauser went public and Chester Taxtrum backed her up. Now it's beginning to rise again."

"How fast?" Nathalie queries. "We only need to hold our lead for the month until the election."

Liz taps more keys. "It's going to be close. We know Schiller's low on money. He's cut back on his rallies and on TV ads. What we're seeing must be the result of his social media strategy. His people are smart. They're making every dollar count."

"Have we got enough funds to counter his push?" Nathalie asks.

"Only if we're at least as smart. But we've still got contributions flowing in, particularly from environmental activists. One of them is a top internet media expert. We can pull her into the fight. And we can put every cent we can spare toward the newest analytics. So whatever Schiller does, we can do it better," Liz assures her boss.

The muscles at Nathalie's jawline pop. "The difference is that what Schiller is selling is pure B.S. He'll say anything that gets him a vote. But we need to convince the public of the truth."

"We will," Liz promises.

Linc's getting to know Rutty's habits pretty well, almost too well. And he's been working on the identity of his pal. So far, he hasn't found any matching pictures. He could try for fingerprints, but he'd need official status to get into the FBI database. And if the mystery man hasn't been picked up for anything, the prints wouldn't be there anyway.

D.N.A. is another matter. If Linc can get a sample, he can submit it to a private lab. He won't get anything out of that but a list of markers. Still, he can work with a specialist in correlating the data with identified individuals. He's known her to suggest possible suspects within a couple of hours. Linc appreciates her as a resource but also finds her success a bit disquieting. These days - even if no crime is involved -

saliva on a water bottle, or a shed hair, can reveal more about a person than they might ever want anyone to know.

Unfortunately, so far, Linc hasn't been able to retrieve anything with the mystery man's D.N.A. on it. So, he's switched from following Rutty to sticking with his unknown subject. But, since he doesn't know his unsub's schedule yet, he can't keep his distance as well as he did with Rutty. That means he'll have to be a lot more careful. To avoid detection, he'll be using several vehicles. He's more comfortable with his own, but the job is the job. At least he's managed to track down the most convenient restrooms in the area. That's something.

While Linc was prepared to lurk around coffee shops and fast-food restaurants to retrieve a discarded drink container, he finally gets a break. When following Rutty's partner-in-crime, he notices a woman engaged in carefully adding a stick-on letter to form the name on a mailbox. As Linc's target pulls into the driveway next to her, she nods a greeting. It couldn't be that easy, could it? Linc circles the block until the woman finishes her task. The investigator regards the final rendering and smiles smugly to himself. "Cookson." While the roster of employees he has for Low-Dunn is largely devoid of pictures, how many Cooksons could there be?

When he has a chance to consult his laptop, Linc discovers that the number of Cooksons at Low-Dunn is far higher than he imagined. Apparently, working for the company is a family affair. He can eliminate the women. But that still leaves five suspects. One by one, he googles them until a winner emerges. There's even a picture. It dates back to Edward (Eddie) Cookson's high school days. Still, his basic features are convincing enough even before Linc runs software to age the image. Merry will have to confirm, but Linc is pretty sure that Eddie Cookson is her second assailant.

"That's the bastard," Merry declares. "So now that we know who he and the other asshole are, what do we do?"

"We don't," Linc responds. "Your lawyers do. They could try to get a D.A. to bring a criminal case or go after those guys civilly. You wouldn't have the satisfaction of seeing your assailants arrested, but a civil case might be the way to go."

"Why?" Merry demands. "I want to see those jerks in jail."

"But you want to go after Ray Schiller even more, don't you?" Linc presses.

Merry's eyes flame. "Damn right!"

"Then if the lawyers do what I think they'll do, they'll use discovery to go after every contact Minger and Cookson have had. So if you're right about Schiller being behind them coming after you, that's where the evidence could be."

"So that's how I'll nail Schiller's ass?" Merry presses.

"It's probably your best option," Linc confirms.

From behind, Liz lays a hand on Nathalie Wellstone's shoulder. "Did you see the latest about Meredith Brookhauser?"

Nathalie whirls around. "No. I've been putting together the message for our volunteers in the field. What happened?"

"She's bringing suit against the two men she claims assaulted her. They both work for Low-Dunn. Her lawyers are going full bore, demanding depositions and discovery. If she's right about the connection to Schiller, that's the best chance we've seen that he'll be exposed for the asshole he is."

"If he ordered Brookhauser's death, he's a lot worse than an asshole," Nathalie mutters. "But we have to hope he's exposed before the election."

"Brookhauser's lawyers are moving fast," Liz notes. "We have a shot."

Graphics flash across the screen as a deep voice announces, "Inflection Point, the venue where we examine the information that pushes controversial cases toward a conclusion. Tonight your host, Ari Melbourne, welcomes the legal panel of Zerlina Vance, Gregory Patrick, and Dan Goldblume. This evening's topic: the alleged involvement of Ray Schiller in the case of Meredith Brookhauser versus Minger and Cookson."

"Mom, it's on! You need to see this," Chester shouts.

"Just a second," Mary yells back. "I'm getting my shoes off. I think we must have knocked on a hundred doors tonight." While Ari is welcoming his guests, she drops on the couch beside her son.

"I believe you've all read the statements from lawyers for Meredith Brookhauser and Low-Dunn, the employer of Minger and Cookson." Ari continues. "While Low-Dunn dismisses Brookhauser's accusations as an extortion attempt, Brookhauser accuses the company of conspiring with Senate candidate Ray Schiller to murder her. Schiller's campaign claims the whole affair is an effort by his opponent, Senator

Nathalie Wellstone, to blacken his good name on the eve of the election. Zerlina, your thoughts."

An attractive woman leans across the table toward the host. "Ari, as I understand it, a sheriff's report documented a soaked Meredith Brookhauser discovered near a lake adjacent to a cabin connected to Low-Dunn. Her lawyers also subpoenaed Rory Montrose, Ray Schiller's campaign manager. According to Brookhauser, Montrose drove her to the cabin. In addition, Montrose is fighting the subpoena. That begs the question of why would Montrose refuse deposition. If he didn't participate in the conspiracy, why not say so?"

"Because merely testifying in a deposition could open him up to perjury charges if he forgets or misstates a fact," Patrick insists.

Goldblume waves his hand dismissively. "The fear of entrapment is a tired dodge. Montrose wouldn't risk perjury charges unless he deliberately attempted to deceive. And if Meredith is lying, he would merely have to tell the truth. The few facts we know so far support Brookhauser's assertions. She has no motive to lie. She's seeking minimal damages in her suit, and a criminal prosecution would engender no monetary gains."

Patrick smacks his palm on the table. "She has the oldest reason in the world to lie, a woman scorned."

"In which case, what she's been saying about Ray Schiller cheating on his wife with her, would be true," Zerlina points out. "And what Chester Taxtrum told the media would also be true. So the one with a motive to lie is the adulterous politician masquerading as a devoted husband. And Nathalie Wellstone has condemned Low-Dunn as an environmental bad actor for years. So the company has every reason to back Ray Schiller's run. So far, the weight of the evidence is on Brookhauser's side."

"However," Ari inserts, "the case is far, perhaps months or years from legal resolution. So the crucial question is, with the election looming, how Ray Schiller will fare against Nathalie Wellstone in the court of public opinion."

"Well, Ari," Goldblume responds, "both candidates have passionate followers. So the messages both parties put out in the last days of their campaigns will be crucial."

Ari turns toward the camera. "And we'll explore those messages after the break."

"Everyone will see what a liar Ray Schiller is," Chester declares, turning from the screen. "Nathalie has to win."

"Chester, you understand better than anyone how convincing Schiller can be," Mary reminds her son. "And you heard Dan Goldblume. Schiller still has a lot of followers who believe in him the way you did. The only way Nathalie can win is if we keep working for her to the last second."

Stretching his tired muscles, Chester regards his mother. "You sound like Liz."

Mary nods in satisfaction. "Good."

CHAPTER TWENTY-ONE

Mary grunts when her cell phone buzzes. She has a lot of territory to cover and not much time to do it. Breath whooshes from her lungs when she sees the caller I.D. It's Doctor Lawrence. She can't hit the green circle fast enough.

"Ms. Taxtrum," Lawrence greets her. "How are you and how is our subject?"

"He's doing great, but we're both swamped trying to keep Nathalie Wellstone in office," Mary confides. "Do you have news about your research?"

"I believe I do," Lawrence replies. "We've observed that certain compounds found in fruits and vegetables seem to have a positive effect in moderating the actions of what we've been calling the believe gene. I wanted to ask you about his diet. I know you told me he thought Schiller was depriving him of food. We've already established that as a stressor. But can you tell me anything in particular that he ate a lot of after he left Schiller's influence?"

Mary shakes her head. "He's never been a big fan of most fruits and vegetables. He ate a lot of pizza."

"Hmm. The tomatoes would have flavonoids and possibly anthocyanins. Both would be good for him, but we've observed the most substantial effects from polyphenols. Was there anything he particularly craved?" Lawrence probes.

"Cherry pie," Mary realizes. "He loves it. For a while, he couldn't get enough."

"That could be it!" Lawrence exclaims. "Cherries are one of the fruits that appear to have the strongest effects."

"Doctor Lawrence," Mary questions, "are you telling me that cherry pie could cure someone with the believe gene?"

"No, Ms. Taxtrum, I'm not saying that, exactly. But I am saying that it could have contributed to more flexible behavior on his part. We'll be continuing to study the matter. In the meantime, you go get 'em for Nathalie Wellstone. If she loses her seat, those of us who dedicate our lives to research will suffer a crippling blow."

Mary nods at her phone. "Getting votes for Nathalie Wellstone is exactly what the subject and I are trying to do."

"Cherry pie!" Lily Rostoff repeats. "Doctor Lawrence said Chester was cured by cherry pie?"

"That's not exactly what he said," Mary recounts. "He thinks that it might have been the cherry pie and maybe some other things like pizza on top of the stress Chester went through working for Schiller. But he's not sure of anything yet."

"But it's possible there might be a cure for our kids, like a cherry pie pill or something?" Lily persists.

"I don't know," Mary admits, "and I don't think Doctor Lawrence does either. He's going to keep doing research. But you might want to watch what Evan eats and how he behaves. We could get the others in the support group to look at stuff like that too. It can't do any harm."

"Except for building up people's hopes." Lily points out.

"There's nothing wrong with hoping," Mary argues. "That's why Chester and I are working so hard for Nathalie Wellstone. We're hoping if she stays in office, she can keep getting scientists like Doctor Lawrence funded."

"I know you are," Lily acknowledges, "but I saw part of a Schiller rally on the news last night. Despite all the stories coming out about him wanting to murder his mistress, the crowd still worshipped him like a god."

"That's because they're believers like Chester was, and Evan and all the other kids of the members of our support group are. That's why Doctor Lawrence's work is so important. It could keep bastards like Schiller from using his lies to grab power. God knows we've got enough of them in government already. With all the craziness out there, this country is a wreck."

Lily sighs. "Do you really think you're going to straighten out the mess with cherry pie?"

"I think," Mary declares, "that it could be a start. And I'm making some before I go on shift tonight. You want one for Evan?"

"I suppose so," Lily considers. "It couldn't hurt."

Mary and Chester stare up at the talking heads from the first row of chairs in front of the Wellstone Headquarters' big screen. The polls closed two hours before, but returns are still coming in with a narrow margin between the candidates.

"Time to go to the big board again," Ari Melbourne announces. "Steve, what have you got for us?"

In his trademark statistics-nerd pants, Steve Koslowski points to numbers appearing as he speaks. "Nathalie Wellstone won this district by 20 points six years ago. But since then, the demographics have changed. She's still showing a considerable lead, but not as large as the one she had before." Again, new numbers appear, and Steve points at a map. "In this district, however, she's outstripping Schiller by a greater margin than she showed against her last opponent."

"How about the exit polls?" Ari inquires.

Steve shrugs. "So far, a dead heat. We're going to have a long night, Ari."

"I'm betting that Nathalie Wellstone and Ray Schiller will have an even longer one," Ari replies. "Thanks, Steve. We'll get back to you in a few moments. Oh, we have some breaking news. The petition to quash Rory Montrose's subpoena to appear in Meredith Brookhauser's suit against her alleged attackers has been denied. If that had happened a few days back, this could have been a different race."

"Damn slow courts!" Liz yells at the screen before noting the disturbed whisperings in the room. "Hang in there," she urges the nervous crowd. "Whatever happens with the accusations against Schiller, Nathalie will win this because of your hard work and because she's the better candidate."

Mary watches the useless crawl across the bottom of the screen. "I hope so," she murmurs.

"What the hell is going on?" Schiller growls in his office at his headquarters. "We were supposed to be winning the rural counties, hands down."

"The numbers didn't say that, Ray," Rory reminds him, "just that we were trending upward. But that was before Wellstone launched her final push. She had her people knocking on every farmhouse door, and she put ads on the organic farming Facebook groups. She was reaching out to the growers who want no part of Low-Dunn. It looks like they came through for her.

"It didn't help us that the Agriculture Committee in the house launched an investigation of Low-Dunn's business practices either. Congressman Farrell went on 'Face the Public' to discuss how Low-Dunn sues farmers trying to grow crops without the company's herbicide-resistant seeds. He ranted about how Low-Dunn goes after them if any pollen drifts over from a neighbor's Low-Dunn plants and made it sound like Low-Dunn preys on the little guys. Worse, your name's been linked with Low-Dunn so much that anyone who sees the company in a suspicious light is skeptical of you. And your alliance with Low-Dunn's put all the tree-huggers in Wellstone's camp too. The Wellstone campaign used social media to mobilize their geeks. We're lucky we're doing as well as we are."

The ice cubes in his double scotch jump as Schiller pounds his fist on the table holding his large screen monitor. "Screw Low-Dunn! They f***ed up everything."

"All the vote's not in yet. We've still got a chance," Rory soothes. "And we've laid the groundwork to challenge the outcome if Wellstone wins."

"Yeah," Schiller acknowledges. "We've already got our people believing she can't beat me unless she cheats. Have you got our backup message ready to launch?"

"As soon as the networks call the race."

CHAPTER TWENTY-TWO

A cheer goes up at four a.m. in Wellstone Campaign Headquarters as a checkmark appears next to Nathalie Wellstone's image on the big screen. Her exhausted body, newly energized, Nathalie walks to the front of the room. Then, with a camera from a reporting pool trained on her, she begins to speak. "The win belongs to each and every one of you, and I can't thank you all enough. Your work has been tireless. And you've persisted in the face of insults and even threats from Schiller supporters. I know what you've been through. I've seen it and heard it. I've felt the sting of malice as Schiller aimed his barrage of lies at every sentence of truth we spoke. But we've brought home the victory.

"I want everyone to soak in this moment, the gratification that flows from overcoming the odds. And then I want you to go home. Get some sleep. Hold your friends and family close. Because this afternoon we're going to celebrate. And then we'll begin the work of turning the promises we made into reality. Again, thank you so much, and I'll see you later."

After exchanging a stream of high-fives and hugs, Mary and Chester make it out the door. "See you this afternoon?" Mary asks before parting from her son.

"I have some hours to make up at work, but I'll be there," Chester promises. "Are you going to bring cherry pie?"

A smile further brightens Mary's already glowing expression. "Of course. How could we celebrate without it? And I can't wait to watch Schiller's concession speech."

"Yeah," Chester agrees. "That will be great."

Mary doesn't bother to shed anything but her shoes before dropping to her bed. Sleep holds her solidly in its grasp for the next seven hours. And when she finally grabs her phone from her bedside table, she sees a YouTube alert. She taps it, eagerly expecting to watch Schiller accept his defeat. His face fills the small screen. "I categorically deny losing this election. The count was a lie and a hoax. My poll watchers have already reported the host of irregularities they witnessed. Nathalie Wellstone has always deceived the good people of this state, and she continued to do so during her entire re-election campaign. But

I know the truth. And after the full recount that I'm demanding, every citizen of this state and of this country will know it too."

A stream of words Mary barely remembers knowing escapes her lips.

Ari Melbourne nods at his guest as the next segment of his afternoon show begins. "Senator Wellstone, thank you for taking the time to join us."

"Thank you, Ari," Nathalie responds. "I appreciate the opportunity to address Ray Schiller's comments about the election."

"Comments is a mild way of putting it," Ari notes. "He accused you of cheating and stealing the vote. He claims that your people collected ballots in rural communities and marked them with votes for you."

"First of all, Ari, that would have been impossible," Nathalie explains. "No one can submit multiple ballots for counting. As you know, it is one person, one vote. If voters vote by mail or drop box, their signatures are checked on each sealed inner envelope. Outer and inner envelopes are bar-coded to avoid duplication. And no one can turn in more than one ballot at the polls."

"He's also accusing you of hacking the voting machines," Ari adds.

A smile quirks Nathalie's lips. "That would be some trick, Ari. The voting machines are air-gapped. They can't be hacked. And the state uses paper ballots. So it will be relatively straightforward for an audit to determine if the results match."

"And will there be an audit?" Ari inquires. "As I understand it, the tally isn't close enough to qualify for a state-funded recount. Will the Schiller campaign be paying for one? Sources say it was running short of funds."

Satisfaction lights Nathalie's face. "To reassure the voters that the election results are trustworthy, we've offered to split the costs of a recount with Ray Schiller's campaign. He has yet to accept our offer, but the ball is in his court."

"She nailed him!" Chester hoots from Mary's couch as Ari goes to break.

"Nathalie called Schiller's bluff," Mary agrees. "But we'll have to see what happens next."

"Recount? What the hell?" Schiller demands. "How is a recount starting so soon? We were supposed to tell my supporters we couldn't afford it and use it to raise money."

"The Wellstone campaign put out enough money to get it going," Rory explains. "After claiming it would show you won, we have no excuse to delay it."

"We have to find an excuse," Schiller insists. "We need to ride that gravy train."

"Well, if you can think of one, you let me know," Rory retorts. "I have my own problems. If I don't give my deposition in Meredith Brookhauser's suit tomorrow, the judge has threatened to hit me with contempt of court."

Schiller shrugs. "Just take the fifth. They can't get you on anything for that."

"Except that everyone who hears about it on the news will immediately assume I'm guilty." Rory shudders. "I can just see Twitter now: 'Rory doesn't roar.' And it isn't just the suit. If the D.A. flips those idiots Minger and Cookson, I could get hauled before a grand jury."

"They're not going to flip," Schiller asserts. "Low-Dunn paid them to stay silent. And if they talk, the company will cut off their families. Just hang on. We've already got the tabloids portraying Meredith as an interloper rejected by a man devoted to his wife. And my followers are lapping it up. Figure out a way to use what Meredith is saying to pull in the bucks we're missing on the recount, and we'll be fine."

"Easy for you to say," Rory throws back. "You weren't the one to drive Brookhauser to the lake. And you weren't the one who got Grover to go to Low-Dunn for help. I have two kids in college, Ray. I can't afford to take the fall for you."

"Just keep your mouth shut at that deposition, and there won't be any fall," Schiller assures his manager. "Get the money flowing into the super PAC, and we'll both be fine."

"Rutty, what are we going to do?" Eddie Cookson worries as he and his cohort await being deposed.

"Just what the lawyer said to do, keep our mouths shut," Rutty declares. "And if anything happens, Low-Dunn will take care of us and our families."

"But that lawyer works for Low-Dunn, not us," Eddie points out. "He'll tell us whatever the company tells him to. And how do we know they'll keep their promises? They already cut back the pension program for the workers who still had one. We got stuck with 401Ks. And since the trouble started with the government, they've stopped their contributions to those too. The big shots could decide to dump all the blame on us and stiff our families. We'd be in prison with nothing we could do while our wives and kids would be out in the cold."

"So, what are you saying?" Rutty demands, "That we should go to the cops or the D.A. or something?"

"Maybe," Eddie considers. "If they cut us a break, at least it will be in writing. Then, we'll be able to count on it. Right now, all we have is the word of a Low-Dunn mouthpiece. How can we go by that?"

Rutty slumps in his seat. "I don't know."

A legal assistant appears and calls from a doorway. "Mr. Minger, we're ready for you."

With his feet dragging along the floor, Rutty follows her.

CHAPTER TWENTY-THREE

Eddie Cookson twitches in his seat next to the attorney he took a second mortgage on his house to hire. "Mr. Cookson, please stand," the judge instructs. "Do you affirm that you've entered into a plea agreement of your own free will and no coercion was employed to obtain your testimony?"

"Uh, yes, Judge, I mean Your Honor."

"And you understand that the terms of your agreement depend on your elocution here today. And that further, any attempt at deception in that elocution will make your plea arrangement null and void, resulting in full charges associated with the crime of attempted murder being brought against you?"

"Yes, Your Honor."

"Then you may begin."

Eddie clears his throat and picks up the sheets of paper holding his statement in a large, easily readable font. "On September 4, 2021, on the instructions of Grover Norliss, Rutherford Minger and I drove to a cabin near Lake Lankershoal. When we arrived, we observed Meredith Brookhauser lying on a bed, apparently unconscious. We put her in a boat on Lake Lankershoal and transported her two miles from the cabin. We attached a weighted belt to her body and threw her into the lake. At that point, we sent a text to a number Norliss gave us, stating 'Job complete.' Following that, we returned to the cabin and retrieved the car we arrived in. Rutherford Minger drove us to Sailorsville, where we both live and work for Low-Dunn. On September 7, 2021, Minger and I returned to work at Low-Dunn with a raise of ten dollars per hour each and promotions to supervisory positions."

Ari Melbourne holds up a Jacob's Ladder toy to the camera as a block appears to flip downward. "You may wonder what a child's plaything has to do with the case against Ray Schiller. Well, unlike the action you've seen here, the flipping of witness after witness has been no illusion. And here to tell you about what happened is the person with the closest involvement: Meredith Brookhauser, whose suit touched off the whole chain of events. Meredith, nice to see you. It's been a while since your last visit."

"Great to be here, Ari. It's been a hectic time."

"Yes, I imagine it has. So let's review it step by step. First, Ray Schiller allegedly conspired to kill you, a crime for which he's now been indicted, based on the testimony of his campaign manager Rory Montrose. But Rory Montrose was the last witness to flip. The first was Edward Cookson, who with Rutherford Minger was recruited from Low-Dunn to drown you in Lake Lankershoal. Have I got that right so far?"

"Yes, you do, Ari. Rory Montrose used Grover Norliss as his go-between to Low-Dunn."

"Got that," Ari acknowledges. "And Norliss flipped after Cookson and Minger. That brought down Low-Dunn CEO Monteith Metzger, who admitted the company's support of Schiller to prevent Nathalie Wellstone from exposing Low-Dunn as a bad actor. So that brings us to Schiller, who claimed no knowledge of the plot to drown you, a claim disputed by Rory Montrose."

"But the cabin Rory drove me to on Lake Lankershoal was used by Schiller for his assignations. Several women have come forward to testify to that," Meredith points out. "It had no connection to Rory Montrose, other than him driving me there. So Schiller is tied into everything. A jury will have to see that."

"Well, we'll find out when he's tried. But we do know one thing. A recount proved that despite Schiller's protests, Nathalie Wellstone was honestly re-elected to the Senate. She continues in her crusade to investigate the actions of Low-Dunn and other potential environmental offenders. We'll be back after this."

I want to welcome everyone to a joint session of the Agriculture, Nutrition, and Forestry Committee and the Commerce, Science, and Transportation Committee," Nathalie Wellstone announces. "This is the first of two hearings we will be holding. Today's witnesses are here to testify to the effect of seeds genetically engineered to resist a Low-Dunn herbicide, on the environment and the economy. Our witnesses are Lee Green for the Organic Farmers Consortium, Curtis Grovington for Farmers' Banking and Loan, and Denver Styles substituting for Monteith Metzger of Low-Dunn.

"Due to time constraints, without objection, we are waving the usual introductions. Those will be available to committee members in writing. Also available to members are the witnesses' opening statements and those of the chairs and ranking members. Each member will be allotted five minutes for questions. A witness responding when a member's time expires will be allowed to complete the answer.

"I will begin by recognizing myself for five minutes. Mr. Green, your opening statement cites 150 members of your consortium driven into bankruptcy by loss of organic status or suits brought by Low-Dunn when seed from their plants was found to have blown over from neighboring fields. Is that correct?"

Green pulls the microphone toward him. "Yes, Senator Wellstone, it is."

"Thank you," Nathalie responds. "Now, Mr. Styles, are you aware that to qualify as an organic grower, farmers can't use genetically modified seed?"

Styles clears his throat. "Yes, Senator."

"Then, would you please explain to me how any organic farmer could possibly prevent contamination with your seed when it is easily carried from their neighbors' acreage by the wind or by animal vectors?"

Styles reaches for a bottle of water and takes a gulp. "I don't know the answer to your question, Senator. Low-Dunn would have to study the problem."

"Mr. Styles, isn't it true that Low-Dunn already conducted such a study and concluded it would be impossible, resulting in Low-Dunn essentially controlling the market?"

Styles gulps more of his water. "I would have to check on that, Senator."

"Do that, Mr. Styles. My committee will expect your answer in writing by the end of this week. Now, Mr. Grovington, how many clients of your institution have been forced to default on their loans due to conflicts concerning Low-Dunn seeds?"

"I don't have the exact numbers, Senator, but well in excess of 50."

Nathalie nods. "And what was the approximate dollar amount of the total of those loans?"

"Fifteen million dollars, Senator."

"And how many of those clients lost their livelihoods?"

"We did the best we could to extend their financing, but in the end, Senator, almost all of them."

Nathalie nods. "Thank you, Mr. Grovington. I yield back the balance of my time."

Chester's pie almost hits the floor as he springs from his chair. "Did you see that? Did you hear what Nathalie did to that jerk from Low-Dunn?"

Mary pours another cup of coffee during a short break in the hearing broadcast on C-Span 2. "I saw it. But Nathalie's fair. I've watched bits of her hearings before. As the chair, she'll give all the other senators a chance to ask questions or just talk for their five minutes. And some of them will be defending Low-Dunn. They've probably been taking the company's money for years and are afraid of losing it."

"They're going to lose it anyway," Chester asserts, "just like Schiller lost in court. I checked. Low-Dunn's stock is going way down. They could go out of business."

"Then some other corporation will buy them cheap and keep trying to sell their products. The only way that won't happen is if Nathalie pushes through legislation to ban what Low-Dunn's been doing. And that won't be easy."

"Well, I'm going to help her any way I can," Chester declares.

Mary brings her coffee to the couch as the hearing resumes. "So will I."

"Are you nervous?" Mary asks as she and Chester wait in an anteroom of a Senate office building.

"Yes," Chester confesses, "but we need to tell our story. Everyone should know how liars like Ray Schiller could take advantage of people like me. So let's do this!"

Nathalie Wellstone smiles from behind the dais in a committee room. "I want to welcome our witnesses to today's hearing of the Health Subcommittee of the Commerce, Science, and Transportation Committee. Today we will be exploring an issue not only vital to the health of our nation but to the democratic process on which it is founded.

"Doctors Lawrence and Greenspan will be discussing their cutting edge research on what they've dubbed the believe gene. In addition, Mary Taxtrum and Chester Taxtrum will be sharing personal testimony of the effects of that gene on their family. At this moment, I will disclose that both Taxtrums were involved with my reelection campaign. However, they were both touched by the effects of the gene long before any research took place. This country owes them both a debt of gratitude for stepping forward to aid in Doctor Lawrence's and Doctor Greenspan's discoveries.

"In the interests of time, without objection, the ranking member and I have declined the opportunity to make opening statements and formal introductions. So, we'll begin with Chester Taxtrum, who has been dubbed by members of the press as 'The Cherry Pie Kid.' Mr. Taxtrum, the country and I are looking forward to hearing you share your story. You may start whenever you're ready."

Chester wraps his fingers around the small water bottle in front of him. "I used to believe a lot of crazy stuff. Those things were bad for me and the country. But I'm better now - as long as my mother keeps baking cherry pies."

9 781949 802306